Does This Book Make Me Look Fat?

Does This Book Make Me Look Fat?

edited by

Marissa Walsh

clarion books • new york

Clarion Books
an imprint of Houghton Mifflin/Harcourt Publishing Company
215 Park Avenue South, New York, NY 10003
Copyright © 2008 by Marissa Walsh

The text was set in 12.5-point Bembo.

www.clarionbooks.com

Printed in the United States of America

Library of Congress Cataloging-in-Publication Data

Does this book make me look fat? / edited by Marissa Walsh.
v. cm.
Contents: Circumferentially challenged / Daniel Pinkwater — Mirror, mirror /
Megan McCafferty — Alterations / Eireann Corrigan — Last red light before we're
there / Matt de la Peña — Sweet 16 plus / Wendy McClure — Some girls are bigger than
others / Sarra Manning — Tale of a half-pint / Margo Rabb — The day before Waterlily
arrived / Jaclyn Moriarty — Hello . . . my name is / Carolyn Mackler — The mating
habits of whales / Barry Lyga ; illustrated by Jeff Dillon — It is good / Sara Zarr —
Pretty, hungry / Ellen Hopkins — How to tame a wild booty / Coe Booth —
Confessions of a former It Girl / Wendy Shanker.
ISBN 978-0-547-01496-8
1. Overweight persons—Literary collections. 2. Body image—Literary collections.
[1. Overweight persons—Literary collections. 2. Body image—Literary collections.]
I. Walsh, Marissa, 1972-
PZ5.D72 2008
[Fic]—dc22
2008025070

MP   10   9   8   7   6   5   4   3   2   1

Beauty is in the eye of the beholder and it may be necessary from time to time to give a stupid or misinformed beholder a black eye.

— Miss Piggy

Contents

Supplements

INTRODUCTION

Take Another Look

Marissa Walsh

I probably ask "Does this make me look fat?" or "Do I look fat?" at least once a day.

Probably more.

I'm not proud of this.

In fact, it gets tiresome, both for me and for those within earshot. Not only does it take a lot of energy, but it annoys me that I'm not thinking about more important stuff. Because I know there are so many better questions I should be asking. Like: How does our friend Barbie actually *stand upright* with her unattainable measurements of 39-21-33? Why has Gwen Stefani been on a diet since the *sixth grade*? And isn't it *sad* that ninety percent of all women ages 15–64 (64!) worldwide want to change at least one aspect of their physical appearance (with body weight ranking the highest)?

Lucky for us, the fourteen writers of all shapes and sizes assembled in these pages have thought about this stuff and written about it here. Some have gotten personal, choosing to share their own true stories with you. Others have taken the fictional path, creating characters we can all identify with and care about.

And hopefully, after you read this book, the next time you're tempted to ask, "Does this book/dress/skirt/shirt/Michelin man costume make me look fat/sticklike/bad/flat chested/stupid?" you'll want to ask, "Who cares?" instead.

I know I'm going to try.

Circumferentially Challenged

Daniel Pinkwater

I'm going to say it! I'm going to say that word—the one you should never say! It can end a friendship. It can cause husband and wife to fight all day. You've got to be careful how you use this word. It's the "F" word. I tell you, it's powerful. Here goes:

Fat. Fat. Fat fat fat. Fat fat fat fat fat. You can't say fat—did you know that? You can say heavy. You can say large. In the case of women you can say full figured or pleasingly plump. I buy my clothes from the Big and Tall shop, or the Mighty Man shop, or I order those attractive fashions that hark back to the early seventies out of the King Size catalog. Never the Fat Man shop. Years ago there used to be a store in New York with a big nineteenth-century-looking sign showing a fat guy in nineteenth-century underwear and bearing the legend IF ALL MEN WERE FAT, THERE WOULD BE NO WARS.

People used to tell it like it was—call a spud a spud. But no more. Saying that someone is fat may be the worst thing one can say. My mother-in-law has often said that she would rather be dead than fat. So far she's neither.

Now, I actually am fat. There's an excellent chance that I am fatter than anybody reading this book. I have been fat all my life, except for a brief period when I was thin, during which I discovered I was still fat, but not physically. I am an authority on being fat. I have experienced most of what a fat person can experience, bad and good—and I have concluded this: It is mostly good.

I'll get the bad part out of the way right now. There is a societal bias against fatness, even though most people in our society are, to some degree, overweight. Fat people are a maligned and oppressed minority.

Big deal. It's very good to be a maligned and oppressed minority. It offers opportunities to develop resilience and tolerance. I'm not suggesting that all fat people are free of prejudice, but maybe more of them than in many groups. You know, "Let him who is without fat cast the first stone."

Then there's the health question. All my life I've been told that, as a fat person, I was at greater statistical risk to develop certain ailments than a thin person. It took me forty years to figure out to ask how much greater a statistical risk. I haven't worried since. If you're overweight, try this: Ask your doctor which would confer the greater benefits: losing weight or quitting smoking, losing weight or exercising more, losing weight or reducing tension.

Being fat has helped me avoid many disagreeable things. As a child, I didn't have to participate in sports, other than when I felt like it. The fact is, many fat people are good athletes, although they should not expect to excel in the track and field category.

I was excused from serving in the military. If George W. Bush and Dick Cheney had been my size at the appropriate time, they would have had nothing to explain later. Incidentally, this is another example of retrograde thinking on the part of society at large. A human tank or a land-blimp battalion would strike terror in the hearts of the enemy—and be very pleasing to view in parades.

Many men dismiss me as nonthreatening because of my globularity, and therefore I get along well with competitive, A-type, killer-instinct, macho individuals—and women love me because I haven't had to develop so many of those unpleasant male traits.

Once I got past believing what other people told me, being spherical has not presented me with many problems. I've been able to do almost everything I've wanted to do. I once climbed Kilimanjaro . . . okay, I didn't get very far, but a lot of thin people don't either. I want to go on record as being a very happy, very fat person.

It's not my purpose to claim that being fat is all beer and Skittles. It's more beer and pizza. Life presents obstacles,-and in my case I actually am an obstacle. In much the same way as I'd rather be rich, or more handsome, I suppose, I'd rather be thin . . . well, maybe not actually thin . . . if I could be any size I wanted . . . I'm thinking now . . . I think I'd rather be the size I am, but with a better wardrobe.

Mirror, Mirror

Megan McCafferty

The Omigoddesses have taken over.

"Omigod you guys," says The Blondest One as she sashays inside and hangs her six items (six is the limit) on a hook. When she speaks, she knows she holds the collective interest of the Ocean County Mall, if not the cosmos, at her mercy. "Which one of these dresses is the *hotnessssssss?*" The sibilance sizzles off her tongue with a crackly snap. Her eyes flicker, flash, and flare in my direction.

"Omigod you guys," wails The Blond One, who follows in behind her. "This is so heeeeeaaaaavy." She is overwhelmed by the six (six is the limit) featherweight faux retrowashed T-shirts folded over the crook of her elbow. She dramatically lurches into the dressing room like a cuter Quasimodo in platform wedgies.

"Maybe it's because those T-shirts outweigh you," offers the third Omigoddess. She is The Least Blond One Who Is Still Fairly Blond but Serves as a De Facto Token Brunette by Comparison. She is reluctantly lugging a pile of denim for The Blond One to try on with her T-shirts. She shuts the door, squeezes past her two friends, and unburdens herself of six pairs of jeans (six is the limit) in various rises and rinses, but just one size, the only negative nonsize that The Blond One has deemed acceptable for trying on today. There is barely enough room to fit one Omigoddess and her six (six is the limit) items, let alone three and eighteen. And yet they insist on this space-invading ritual, even though the crossing of physical boundaries will inevitably lead to transgressions of the emotional kind.

The Blondest One shoves her wrist under The Blond One's nostrils. "Did you smell this? It's so scrummy!" When The Blond One cringes and refuses to inhale, The De Facto Token Brunette gamely volunteers to take a whiff.

"Who is that one again?"

"Logan," answers The Blondest One, holding up the bottle of cologne ostensibly named after the anonymous, headless model whose chiseled torso is featured on the label.

"I thought it was Hunter," says The De Facto Token Brunette.

"No," says The Blondest One with an emphatic head shake. "Hunter smells like sugar cookies and fresh-cut grass. Logan smells . . ." She sniffs again and swoons. "Like cinnamon. . . ."

"And sex!" blurts The De Facto Token Brunette, making The Blondest One giggle.

"Logan smells like donuts," murmurs The Blond One with a grimace. "He smells like cinnamon-powdered donuts."

The Blondest One presses her wrist to her own pert nose and snorts. "Omigod! You're totally right!"

"I wouldn't mind having either one of them on me . . . ," says The De Facto Token Brunette, waggling her eyebrows. The Blondest One gives her a forceful but affectionate shove.

I wish I had a nose so I could join in on the fun.

"If I can't get into these jeans," says The Blond One, directly addressing the denim, her face reddening at the very idea, "I'll never. Eat. Anything. Again."

"I'll never cure polio," says The De Facto Token Brunette.

The other two Omigoddesses pretend not to hear her.

"It's not a big deal," says The Blondest One to The Blond One in a flat tone that doesn't even try to sound sincere. "Maybe you should try on a few pairs in the next size up. . . ."

The Blondest One has barely shifted her gaze from me—or rather, herself—since she stepped inside the dressing room. She puckers her lips, fluffs her hair, sucks in what little there is of her stomach. I'm used to this, the preening, the posing, the pretending. I want to tell this girl that she is very pretty indeed, but the more she worries about her appearance, the less attractive she seems to others.

I want to tell her, but I can't. I don't have a mouth. I am nothing more than a plane of smooth, polished glass coated in a metal amalgam that reflects an image of the beholder. Or beholders, as the case may be, during particularly hectic shopping seasons.

To protect the privacy of the underage and under-dressed, I can't reveal the name of the store in which I hang. Maybe I *do* grace the inside of the dressing room at Hollister. But I could just as easily be found inside Hot Topic, Urban Outfitters, dELiA*s, Forever 21, Charlotte Russe, or none of the above. For the sake of clarity, I'll call this store X Brand. The X Brand goal is to be the label of choice for **classic/edgy ★ sexy/sweet ★ knowing/naive** tweens and teens. Really, all you need to know is that if you are a female between the ages of twelve and twenty, you almost certainly own at least one item of clothing from X Brand. You're probably wearing an X Brand cami or mini *right now*.

X Brand is designed to look and sound like a velvet-rope club, not a department store. That's why the X Brand soundtrack is played so eardrum-bumpingly loud over the sound system that one must shout in order to be heard. There is no such thing as quiet conversation, so I hear everything.

"Easy for you to say," The Blond One says to The Blondest One after a blast of emo-pop keening. "You eat whatever you want and never get fat."

A brief but unmistakable smile crosses The Blondest One's face before she screws it up into a show of disgust. "Are you kidding?" The Blondest One nips at her waist with her fingertips and points to the flesh caught in her manicured calipers. "I'm so bloated." From my vantage point she does not appear to be carrying an extra micro ounce of bloat. "I don't even know why I'm trying anything on today," she continues. "I'm just torturing myself."

"I eat whatever I want," points out The De Facto Token Brunette with a smirk and an arch of her eyebrow.

I want to cheer for her. *She* knows that a life without donuts is not a life at all. Hooray! The Omigoddesses feel otherwise. They swivel their golden tresses in her direction and assume a look of mock admiration.

"Yes, you do," The Blondest One says simply, restraining herself from finishing the sentence.

The Blond One has no such self-censoring mechanism. "And that's why you'll never fit into these jeans," she says, pointing to the stack on the floor.

"I don't want to fit into those jeans," The De Facto Token Brunette says drily. "I like my jeans. I like my *genes*." The homophonic difference is lost on her friends, but not on me. I wish I could tell her.

"Yay for you!" says The Blond One, clapping like the cheerleader she once was, before she gave it up to spend more efficient calorie-burning hours at the gym. I'd join in the celebration, if I had hands. "But you know what? I *do* want to fit into these jeans. And I *don't* eat whatever I want so I will!"

I try not to be crushed by The Blond One's sarcasm.

"And if they don't fit?" asks The Blondest One, still looking at herself.

"That's not an option today," The Blond One says.

"It's not a big deal," The Blondest One repeats. "*I'm* not a size negative zero. I'll *never* be a size negative zero."

I wish I could say that The Blondest One had announced this seriously, solemnly, as if taking a vow: *I'll never be a size negative zero.* But her wistful tone revealed a rare moment of weakness for this Omigoddess, the one universally acknowledged as the most popular and most powerful, who, despite her peerless status, still compares herself unfavorably to The Blond One in all matters that relate to diet and weight. The Blond One simply has more masochistic willpower than she does.

"I'll never be the first person to land on the moon," says The De Facto Token Brunette.

The Blondest One huffs and tilts her head in the general direction of The De Facto Token Brunette. "Okay. You win. I'm going to ask. What are you babbling about?" The Blondest One almost hisses, but doesn't quite. Her tone is weary, barely tolerant, but not yet totally pissed off. The De Facto Token Brunette often makes The Blondest One laugh, which is why she likes having her around. The De Facto Token Brunette is also two inches shorter and ten pounds heavier than she is, two factors that make it much easier to enjoy her jokes. However, she senses that The De Facto Token Brunette might be making fun of her at the moment, but she hasn't quite figured out how.

"I will never win the gold medal for women's figure skating in the 1976 Olympics," says The De Facto Token Brunette. "Idigi widigill nidigevidiger tridiganslidigate thidige Idigillidigiidigad idigintidigo gidigibberish . . ."

"Okay, I get it," The Blondest One says, surrendering

to laughter. "These are all impossible things you will never do."

"And I'll never be a size negative zero," says The De Facto Token Brunette with all the solemnity lacking in The Blondest One's earlier proclamation.

The Blond One blinks at the other two with pity, because it's true: Neither The Blondest One nor The De Facto Token Brunette will ever be size negative zeroes, not even close. The Blondest One catches The Blond One's pinched, patronizing expression and can't recall why she tolerates her presence, especially when The Blond One is two inches taller and ten pounds thinner than she is.

The Blond One opens her wide, thin-lipped mouth to speak. "Omigod." She sighs and unloads her featherweight faux retrowashed T-shirts onto the floor, then curls herself into the opposite corner of the bench, eyes closed, hand pressed to forehead, pretending to recover from her arduous five-second journey from the shop floor to the dressing room. "Omigod," she repeats, because no one has reacted to her feint fainting spell. "Those shirts were so *heeeeaaaaavy*."

"It wasn't funny the first time," The Blondest One says, wrinkling her nose in disdain, suddenly remembering why she keeps The Blond One around: To subjugate in all matters except diet and weight.

"Seriously," agrees The De Facto Token Brunette as she takes out her multifunctional handheld communication device and starts thumbing away.

Sometimes I feel like the know-it-all older sister, who wants to encourage The Blond One to build up lean muscle mass by adding strength training to her cardio, or warn The Blondest One that every time she wrinkles her face like that, she looks just like her mother, or explain to The De Facto Token Brunette that the thumbs are not particularly dextrous digits and she's at risk for repetitive-strain injuries. It's a good thing I can't say these things, because if I could, and did, they certainly wouldn't want me hanging around them anymore.

But I know the Omigoddesses well enough to *want* to tell them these things. They spend almost every Saturday afternoon here at X Brand, trying on and taking off clothes. I know that they are all juniors at the local public high school, and I know that they are popular enough at this high school to get frequent invitations to various formals, semiformals, and unformals, all of which require new looks from head to toe. This week they are here to buy outfits for a party being held at the home of a fourth Omigoddess who occasionally joins them on these shopping expeditions, though not today. These three are united, in part, by their intense dislike of The Fourth One. They are willing to overlook The Fourth One's faults because her parents often travel on the weekends. Apparently, unsupervised parties are optimal for getting buzzed and brave enough to flirt with the cutest boys.

Fortunately, on most weekends they only *pretend* to get drunk. I've heard The De Facto Token Brunette disavow underage drinking because it (a) is illegal, (b) impairs judgment, and (c) inflicts damage on vital organs. The Blondest One abstains because she usually doesn't need to resort to such desperate boy-getting ploys. The Blond One knows even *lite* beer, even rum and *Diet* Coke, even vodka and *sugarfree* Red Bull have about a hundred empty calories per drink, and those calories usually contribute to unfortunate and unattractive bloating of the abdominal and/or facial regions.

The Blond One decides it's time to see if all her teetotaling, exercising, and meal skipping have paid off. She is ready to try on the six pairs of jeans in the only negative nonsize that The Blond One has deemed acceptable for trying on today. She plans to wear them with the featherweight faux retrowashed T-shirts silk-screened with the names of bands she's barely heard of.

"Oooooh, *Blondie*," she says, admiring the image of a poster commemorating a tour completed ten years before she was born. "Like me!" I want to tell her that she looks very pretty in pink—it brings out a cheerful flush in her cheeks that I rarely see otherwise. She's about to take off the featherweight faux retrowashed T-shirt she bought last week when she focuses her jade green contact lenses on The De Facto Token Brunette, who hasn't ceased texting since she sat down. "Put the camera away before I get naked!"

The other Omigoddesses roll their violet and aquamarine contacts. "Get over yourself," The Blondest One says as she unshyly shimmies out of one synthetic fabric and into another. "Anyone who wants to see you naked already has."

"Seriously," The De Facto Token Brunette says before continuing to thumb away in defiance. "And nude photo Internet scandals are *so* mid-00s."

The Blond One is silent, her peevish lips curling in on each other as she watches The Blondest One's head disappear through the bottom of a spandex tube dress. Her mouth rearranges itself into a smile as her friend snakes her way through the top of the unforgiving, unflattering fabric.

"That is the hotnessssss!" The Blond One lies.

The Blondest One ignores her and turns to The De Facto Token Brunette. "What do you think?" She twirls and pivots, seeking her approval.

The De Facto Token Brunette barely looks up from the tiny screen. "Wow."

"'Wow' good? Or 'wow' bad?"

"Wow as in: 'Wow. I never thought that you could look *that* not hot.'"

I agree with The De Facto Token Brunette's assessment. If I were the one to break this news, I would quickly follow it up with a more positive message. At least this proves that no one looks good in everything. Right? *Right?*

The Blondest One furiously yanks the dress over her head and throws it on the floor. "Ugh! I'm so bloated! I'm hideous!"

"The *dress* is hideous," The De Facto Token Brunette reasons as she picks it up off the floor and clips it back to its hanger. "*You* are the hotnessssss. No one looks good in everything. . . ."

That's exactly the point I would have made!

"I liked the dress." The Blond One's lie is more transparent than any featherweight faux retrowashed T-shirt she will try on today.

"I'm not even going to dignify that lie with a reply."

"What does that even mean?" The Blond One asks.

"It means she's *not even going to dignify that lie with a reply,*" explains The De Facto Token Brunette, slowly, carefully, as if talking to someone who has just woken up from a prolonged coma. "Which in itself is a reply. . . ."

"I'm out," The Blondest One announces, holding up her palms in surrender. "I'm not trying anything else on today. I'll never try on anything ever again."

"I'll never *base* jump from the roof of the Ocean County Mall," muses The De Facto Token Brunette.

"Can I borrow your unused parachute to wear to the party? It will be the only thing that fits!" The Blondest One grabs the offending dress along with the five untried-on items. "Ugh! PMS!" She sniffs her wrist. "Meet me at the Food Court when you're done here. I'll be wallowing in a trough of Papa D's Donuts." She swings open the dressing room door and lets it slam behind her. When The Blondest One's hormonally charged hysterics can no longer be heard, The Blond One speaks up.

"Omigod," she gasps. "What. A. Bitch."

"Um, okay," says The De Facto Token Brunette, used to The Blond One's tirades.

"Seriously," she says. "She's such an underminer. She knows I have a weakness for Papa D's Donuts. If she comes back here with a bag of donuts, I will have to kill her with my bare hands."

"You're worn out from carrying a six-ounce stack of T-shirts. You're not killing anyone."

"She doesn't want me to fit in these jeans."

"Maybe she wants what's best for you."

I was thinking the same thing. That maybe, just maybe, The Blondest One is concerned about The Blond One's obsession with shrinking down to the smallest of negative nonsizes. If that's the case, why can't The Blondest One just come out and say she's worried about her, without being so passive aggressive and . . . um . . . *bitchy?*

"Yeah, right." The Blond One blows an amused raspberry. "She just doesn't want me to be skinnier than she is."

I fear that The Blond One might be onto something there. . . .

"You're already skinnier than she is. You're skinnier than the poster kids for Oxfam."

"I am?" The Blond One's features soften for the first time all afternoon. "That's so sweet."

"I'm not trying to be sweet, I'm trying—"

"Sweet. Omigod! If she comes back here smelling all donutty . . ." She balls her fists in fury. "Omigod! I have not worked this hard to be undone by a bag of donuts!" She picks up a pair of jeans in the only negative nonsize deemed worthy of trying on today and then . . . paralysis.

"Are you going to try those on or what?" asks The De Facto Token Brunette, pointing to the pile of denim.

The Blond One looks stricken. "I don't know."

"What do you mean you don't know?" asks The De Facto Token Brunette.

"I'm scared," she whimpers.

"You're scared," deadpans The De Facto Token Brunette.

"Seriously," says The Blond One, totally, totally serious. I can see the genuine fear in her eyes, beneath the fake jade irises.

"Scared of what?'

"Scared they . . ." She chokes, unable to bring herself to complete the sentence.

"Won't fit?"

The Blond's contacts pop. She barely recovers, then nods wordlessly.

I want to tell her that she should be more scared about what will happen if they *do* fit.

"You should be more scared of what will happen if they *do* fit," says The De Facto Token Brunette.

"What?" asks The Blond One.

"If they fit . . . then what?" asks The De Facto Token Brunette.

Whoa . . . that's what I was thinking! Freaky.

"Then I wear them to the party and I'm the hotnesssssss!"

"Okay," says The De Facto Token Brunette. "Then what?"

"What do you mean, then what?" asks The Blond One, baffled. "Then . . . um, I wear them . . ."

"Then you wear them and you're the hotnessssssss for, like, a day. Maybe a week or two. . . ."

Freeeeeeaky. This has never happened before! The De Facto Token Brunette is taking the words right out of my mouth. Um, that is, if I had one.

"But then that familiar sense of emptiness sets in," continues The De Facto Token Brunette, saying the words I cannot say. "And it's not just the emptiness in your stomach. It goes deeper. Much deeper. Deep, deep down, you'll realize you're not any different than you were when you were a regular zero, or a two, four, six, eight, ten, twelve, fourteen, or whatever you were when you started on your starvation diet."

"So?"

"When does it end?" asks The De Facto Token Brunette. "When you . . ."

Disappear?

". . . disappear?"

The Blond One narrows her eyes at The De Facto Token Brunette. "Omigod," she says derisively. "I had no idea that Eating Disorder Awareness Month came early this year."

"Look," says The De Facto Token Brunette. "I'm just trying to help you—"

"You're just trying to help me stay fat," she seethes, tossing the jeans to the floor and stomping out of the dressing room without taking it or her other untried-on items with her. "Underminer!"

The De Facto Token Brunette rises from the bench, pulls the door shut, and twists the lock with a satisfying click. Eyes closed, she slides down the door and onto the floor with a sigh. A minute goes by, maybe two, until she reaches for the discarded denim, folds it carefully, and adds those jeans to the rest of the stack. Then she picks herself up off the carpet, stands before me, and peers so intently that I swear she's searching for something beyond her own reflection. Is she?

Can you hear me?

The De Facto Token Brunette takes a step forward, coming so close that her breath fogs the glass, concealing her image.

You tried to help. Don't give up.

She wipes the haze away with one of the featherweight faux retrowashed T-shirts, then takes a step backward to reassess what she sees.

And don't give in, either.

The De Facto Token Brunette lifts her chin, lengthens her torso, leads with her cleavage, and smiles.

Be kind to one another. Be kind to yourselves. Do you hear me? Do you . . . ?

"Omigod!"

The De Facto Token Brunette instinctively flinches. The Omigoddesses' chitchattering clatter has shattered this brief moment of clarity. Her smile fades, her body droops.

"I'll never be one of them," she whispers.

Is that a promise? Or a regret? I can't tell.

The Blondest One tugs on the door handle and is shocked to discover that it's locked.

"Omigod!" wails The Blond One. "Open up!"

The De Facto Token Brunette smiles wanly, her hand hovering over the latch as she debates whether she will let the Omigoddesses back in.

Alterations

Eireann Corrigan

It takes two people to zip me into my wedding gown. At the last fitting, my sister had to tug the bodice together, while the seamstress eased up the zipper. Then I slowly edged over to the mirror and spent five tense minutes forcing myself to look at my reflection. For the past few months I'd pictured myself looking like a giant marshmallow in the dress. No one could convince me to try it on. I refused to keep it in my own closet. I tried to convince Jeff to take it, but he's one of those old-fashioned grooms. So first it hung next door, at my friend Shawn's house. Then it traveled to my sister Maureen's. I kept one picture of it taped to the control panel of my treadmill, and another hung on my refrigerator door. Other than that, the dress didn't exist. I refused to discuss it with anyone.

I bought the gown over a year before at a sample sale in the city. My friend Nina and I waited in line for two hours to tear through the store with fifty other women with diamonds winking from their fingers. Because it was so crowded, the saleswomen crammed two brides into each fitting room, and it was the girl sharing my room who tried on the gown first. She was so tiny, the saleslady had to use clips to tighten the satin around her waist. Nina nodded toward the gown while the other girl twirled in front of the mirror. I considered the simple silhouette, the V-neck, and the constellations of dark pearls embroidered across the waist. "Yes," I mouthed to Nina. She narrowed her eyes, and when the girl ultimately shrugged and shook the dress off, we pounced. As soon as the girl stepped out of the gown, Nina helped me pull it over my body.

It was fantastic—exactly what we'd been looking for: mostly classic, with the dark beadwork making it memorable. No long train or anything else princessy. Not at all poofy. And about two sizes too small.

The lady didn't need to bust out her clips on my behalf. We didn't even try to zipper it. We oohed and ahhed, and the saleslady reminded me that most brides lose weight before the wedding. "From the stress." She diagnosed it emphatically in her Eastern European accent. "Do you tend to eat less when you are busy, nervous?"

"Yes." I said it carefully, still measuring myself in the mirror.

"How long do you have until the wedding?"

"A little over a year. I'd probably need to lose twenty pounds."

"Fifteen—but I think you can do this. Do you find it difficult to lose weight?"

And then Nina dissolved. I shook a little, stifling a laugh. The woman must have thought we were lunatics.

Nina managed to get out, "She wrote the book on it." And we kept laughing all the way through negotiating a better sale, turning over my credit card, watching the ladies wrap the dress in tissue and pack it up for me to take home.

When Nina and I first met, losing twenty pounds might have killed me. I don't mean that in an it-would-have-been-a-frustrating-and-arduous-endeavor way. I mean I'd just gotten off tube feedings. My weight was somewhat stable but still almost thirty-five pounds short of the number that the doctors on the eating disorder ward demanded I reach. I was an expert at the psych-treatment tango; I'd eat to force the scale up enough for everyone to feel comfortable sending me off to college. Then I'd drop weight pretty much as soon as my parents unloaded the minivan. But I was an ardently apologetic anorexic. I attended my group therapy meetings religiously and read poem after poem about my recovery in the student pub.

My eating disorder had started around my sixteenth birthday. It was like a tornado tore through and afterward nothing looked the same. By the time I recognized myself again, eight years had passed. I spent almost two of those years in treatment facilities. I'd done irreversible damage to my kidneys, developed a heart murmur, and pretty much torpedoed any chance of conceiving children. Anorexia is not like mono—you don't just suddenly catch it. It's not the flu or even the clap. It looked like I'd suddenly gotten obsessed with food, but the truth was I'd never felt comfortable in my body. There was the time I realized that every other girl in the fourth grade could turn a cartwheel. And the three months spent sipping Slim-Fast in the sixth grade. There was the sweatsuit that I hated—gray with neon triangles all over it. I agonized over wearing that thing, convinced that it made me look fat. A couple weeks ago my mom and I sifted through baby pictures for a wedding day slide show. I found one of the Dread Gray Sweatsuit. "How old was I here?" I tapped the picture of the skinny blond kid with her arms folded across her chest.

And she said, "Six."

So it took me almost a decade to get sick. It's not like I suddenly got better. And usually when I said I was better, I was lying.

Sometimes I was making myself throw up. Before that I was burning myself with an electric iron, searing a pattern of scars into my skin. They're keloid scars—raised and white because I'd keep opening up the same marks after they'd scabbed and healed. It amazes me now—the patience with which people treated me. No one interrupted my lengthy lectures on my recovery to point out that my arm was probably infected. No one took me by the shoulders and shook.

In the hospital they teach you over and over again—eating disorders aren't about being thin. They're about creating this whole world that's so busy counting out the calories in green beans, there's no time to focus on facts of your life that might hurt you. Back then I thought that was horseshit. Really, I'd want to say: Just tell me how many calories you burn by jiggling your foot like this. But hour after hour I sat in various calming offices, hashing out the minute details of my determination to damage myself. I didn't know it because I had slick therapists, but little by little, my head swiveled in the right direction.

By the time my first book, *You Remind Me of You,* came out, words like "recovery" and "health" were more than just the language of wishful thinking. Publishing it dared me to live up to all my tough talk. I hadn't just announced my intentions to stay well at the family dinner table. I'd put out a book about them. Almost as soon as the book hit the stores, the e-mails landed in my inbox. From thirteen-year-olds and thirty-nine-year-olds. Men and women. That book mattered to people in a way that shocked me and thrilled me and made it completely impossible to let my stupid old tricks make a liar out of me.

It wasn't that there weren't bad days. Or even bad months. And as aware as I was that there were people at book readings looking to see if I was still healthy, I also knew there were others checking to see that I was still thin. A friend found a thread started on a pro-ana website. Someone had posted my author shot and started a debate about whether or not I had "let myself go." We laughed about it, but it sickened me a little—picturing some unhealthy girl at her desk measuring the fullness of my face with her thumbnail.

No one gasps anymore when they look at me. If that means I've let myself go, then I'm okay with that. When people see me now, they might not guess my medical history. It's been a few years since I've had that old sunken-cheek pallor. Probably my scarred arm signals some difficult past, but that's it. When I speak at schools or Girl Scout troops or libraries, I want my recovery story to ring true and my advice to count as legitimate. The power to scare people with your own visible skeleton is a sad and desperate power, and that's ultimately what I had to let go. But my voice is strong enough now. I don't need to spell things out on my body.

Just like there are all sorts of tricks to getting sick, there are all sorts to getting well. Throwing out the scale, getting a manicure every week, imagining how horrific it would be to let a little kid live on diet soda and skinless chicken. Then treating yourself with the same gentle care. For me, though, it came down to a very simple fact: Other things finally became more important. Writing and teaching, the play I directed, my friends and family. And now the life I'm beginning with Jeff.

Still. I didn't want to begin that life as a giant marshmallow. Regardless of my steadfast march toward good health, there's still a part of me that panics when my clothes feel tight. I have a list of words in my head—pudgy, plump, chubby, chunky—and I don't want to be described as any of them. Sometimes even the word "healthy" still hurts.

The fall of my first hospitalization, our school drama club put on a play about a restaurant. I played a writer who wouldn't eat. We didn't know then that it was typecasting.

We used my oldest sister's prom dress for my costume, and when I first tried it on, it was too snug. So I lost weight. And then it hung too loosely, so the cast mom who tailored our costumes took it in. So then I lost more weight. And then she took it in again. I chased that dress for months that way, through almost forty pounds.

I know that when my parents and sisters saw my wedding gown and the determined look on my face, they also saw that amazing, shrinking, gauzy, blue dress. Even I was afraid. I am an encyclopedia of relapse and recovery data. Major life changes trigger eating disorders. Feeling "on-stage" spurs on anorexia. There are workouts called "Buff Brides" and weight-loss groups devoted to pre-wedding weight loss. And there I was wading in.

So I didn't try on the dress for a year. I started lifting weights and cut down on sugar and white flour. Back in the nineties I got sick during the fat-free kick and mostly ate rice and bagels. So none of my new protein-crazy meals reminded me of ye olde days of self-inflicted famine. I covered the calorie counter on my new treadmill with duct tape. And then I just ran.

Since college I had been afraid to exercise. It always got out of hand. At Sarah Lawrence I'd been banned from the fitness center for abusive use of the StairMaster. There weren't even sneakers in my closet for years.

Lately, though, I have learned to love the way my body moves—running for ten miles at a stretch and sprinting at ten miles an hour. My legs are hard; I can flex them and see cables of muscles. This summer I swam laps until my limbs could cut through the water like precision blades. Remember when you were a little kid and still impressed with all the stuff you could make your body do? You could kick *that* high. You could stomp *that* hard. You could stretch and, holy cow, you could reach the top shelf of your closet with the tip of your finger. That's how it's been every day—running through the woods behind school, or on the towpath along the river, even just on the repeating rubber track of the treadmill.

When I eat, I fill my plate with fuel and know that my food will boost me toward the new things I want to try. Scuba diving and spelunking. Boxing and rock climbing. My weight has dropped, but not by a lot. I don't think. I haven't weighed myself in this millennium. I'm faster, though, and not such a wuss about pushing open heavy glass doors. A few people have complimented me on losing weight.

And that was weird.

It's been years since I've been a part of that club. Not since the summer of 1993, when I first started dieting. After that, no one uttered the sentence "You've lost weight" without a note of disapproval or even panic in their voice. So this winter when people praised me, I felt myself go cold and tense with shame. *What did I look like before? How did people stand to look at me?* That's crazy talk, obviously—the kind that would have won me a shrink session in previous circles. But it's there.

These days I just lace up my sneakers and run away from it.

In exactly one week I'm going to step into my wedding gown for the last time. I'm not worried. It's an amazing dress. And at that last fitting, when I finally raised my eyes to my reflection, it looked amazing on. There might even be gasps when I walk down the aisle, but not from uneasy people ready to sign me over for tube feeding. No one will be staring at my scarred arm. No one will be thinking about the old blue dress I wore in the school play.

Except me. I found it wadded in a box with my old yearbooks and a disintegrating prom corsage. I cut out a square of it and asked the seamstress to sew it into the hem. All at once, it's my something old, borrowed, and blue. It's old enough that the fabric has faded, but it's still a hazy, filmy blue. And I've borrowed it from that other girl who wore it years ago, the one who swayed onstage and hated the way it gathered against her waist. I've finally outrun her. Honestly? She eats my dust.

Last Red Light Before We're There

Matt de la Peña

For Emily

Moms broke down on the phone last night, talking all crazy about what it felt like to have her only son grow up and move away. "You don't know what it's like, though, Chico. Imagine somebody just came in your dorm room while you were sleeping and snuck your favorite high-tops so you couldn't play ball no more. It's like that, *mijo*. Only worse. And just so you know, this has absolutely nothing to do with your sister. Ana's gonna be just fine. I promise you." At that point she stopped talking and started breathing quicker. Like she always does when the subject of Ana comes up. We sat there in silence for a good half minute, me picturing her frowning brown face as she sat at the kitchen table with the cordless, alone. Fighting tears. Trying to figure out for the thousandth time that day where she'd gone wrong.

Sometimes when I think of my moms like this, alone and brokenhearted, pleading with her own kid to come home, it makes me feel like I'm floating floating floating. Like my entire body has just lifted out of whatever chair I was sitting in and is now hovering in the air like a helium balloon, like a glimmering bubble some kid at the park has blown through an oversized bubble wand. Then *pop!* I drop back into my seat.

I stuffed all my well-rehearsed excuses back in my pocket and switched the phone from one ear to the other. "All right, Ma," I said. "I'm comin' home then. I'll talk to Coach and catch the morning bus, and I'll see you tomorrow afternoon."

She blew her nose into the phone. "You'd really do that, Chico? You'd come all the way down here just to celebrate with your lonely ol' mom?"

"Of course I would, Ma. I'll see you tomorrow, all right?"

"Oh, *mijo,* you don't know how much this means. Not just to me, but *everybody*. The whole family. I'll have Reina pick you up in her car. And we'll make a nice big party for you. How's that sound?"

"Come on, Ma. You know I don't need no party—"

But she'd already hung up. *Of course* there would be a party for my birthday. That's the way it is with my family. They'll use any excuse in the book to get together for a cooler of ice-cold beer, Uncle Ferni's blended margaritas, Aunt Reina's hot-off-the-griddle tortillas, and my gramma's world-famous tamales. Even with my sis sick like she is—for a few hours at least we'll still be laughing and eating and cracking jokes on each other.

The last time I saw Ana was right here at my college. For her sixteenth birthday everybody in the family pooled their money together and bought her a plane ticket to come see me. One of my assistant coaches drove me to the airport to pick her up, and then he dropped us off at a Mexican restaurant just off campus, and after we wolfed down empanadas with meat and potatoes, we crossed the street and had the best frozen yogurt in all of Stockton. Then we went back to the dorms to shower and change clothes (I sent her down to the girls' floor), and I dragged her to this big party at the rich-kid fraternity. I even let her share a few sips of my second beer.

Ana's always looked up to me—that's how it is, I guess, when you're somebody's big brother—but on her trip up to Stockton she saw me in a whole new light. I'm on a basketball scholarship, so a lot of people know me and invite me to random parties because they think it's important to have a couple guys from the "hoop squad" in the house. When we walked in, every other dude we passed shouted, "Hey, yo, Chico!" or "Chico, my man!" or they'd just slap my hand and pull me in for a little halfhearted dude hug. And the girls. Man, I can't tell you how many girls came up to us that night. Blonds, brunettes, Mexicans, Asians, freshmen, juniors, rich girls, tall girls, you name it. "This your little sister, Chico?" they'd say in that singsongy voice girls like to put on (and they'd say it like Ana wasn't standing right there with us). "She's absolutely *adorable.* Look at this beautiful thick brown hair. And these dimples. And she's so thin. What are you, honey, a size *zero?* God, Chico, I'd absolutely kill to have my body look like hers again."

I know what you're thinking: a Mexican playing college basketball? You probably think I should be kicking around a soccer ball or spending five nights a week in the cafeteria on some work-study setup. But I'm six foot three with mad quicks. I can shoot threes for days. And when I realized my moms didn't pull in enough *scrilla* to help me with college, I made it my goal to get a scholarship. Practiced day and night for three, four straight years. During my senior season Coach put in a few calls to scouts he knew, and some of them came to watch me play. The rest is history. Here I am. A Mexican point guard getting respectable burn as a freshman.

On *and* off the court (if you get what I'm sayin').

Anyway, when me and Ana left the party, we went back to my dorm, ordered a pizza, and stayed up late-night talking about what it's like to be in college.

"And you don't have to go to bed at any certain time?" Ana said, pulling a slice of pepperoni out of the box and plopping it down on her paper plate.

"Nope."

"And you can just have anybody spend the night? Whenever you want?"

"Yep."

"And all those people we were with, they hang out and party like that every night?"

"Pretty much."

"Man, Chico," she said with her mouth half full, "I'm gonna go to college, too. I swear to God." She dabbed a folded napkin against a fresh slice to pull off the extra grease and then looked up at me, her big brown eyes lit up like a buzzing deli sign. "Hey, Chico, maybe I could even get in *here*. I could live right downstairs from you, where I took a shower, and we could go to all them parties together, and I could meet tons of friends because everybody loves you and you're my big brother so they'd have to love me, too."

She paused for a couple seconds to think about what she'd just said. "Or would that make you mad, Chico? Having your kid sister following you all around like a little puppy dog?"

"Heck no," I snapped back, tossing a piece of crust back into the pizza box. "It'd be perfect. Then I could make sure no punk-ass dudes try and step to you."

She laughed, but I wasn't joking. I was never cool with the idea that dudes (maybe even shady ones like the guys on my hoop team) would eventually turn their bull-crap raps on my little sis. Actually, it made me pissed off just thinking about it.

Ana wiped her mouth with a napkin and looked at the TV for a sec. But I could tell she wasn't really *looking* at it. She was working something out in her head. "Hey, Chico," she said after a minute or so. "You know all those girls that kept coming up to us at the party?"

"What about 'em?"

"Well, I was just thinking. How come none of them are your actual girlfriend?"

"I like to keep my options open," I said, reaching for my basketball. I spun it on my index finger, and we both watched it rotate around and around at the speed of light.

"What does *that* mean?"

"Well, Michele's cool. But she wanted a relationship. And Mary was fun for a few weeks at the start of the season, until she put on the freshman fifteen. And Sarah's all right, except her forehead gets mad shiny whenever it's a hot day. And this one time I caught Amanda wearing damn flip-flops with socks. Which ain't cool, by the way, Ana. Don't ever do that."

"God, Chico, what do these girls up here gotta do for you to really like 'em?"

"Easy," I said, tucking the ball under my arm. "Be a perfect ten." We both laughed, and Ana turned back to the TV. But she still wasn't watching.

We stayed up most of that night talking, and then the next day I took her on a tour of the campus and at night she sat in the crowd with everybody else and watched us storm back from fifteen down to beat Fresno State in the final seconds. I didn't start, but I came off the bench to score eight points including two three-pointers in the second half. After the game we went to this volleyball girl's house party, hung out some more, and then cruised back to my dorm, where we crashed right in front of the TV in our street clothes. The next day my coach drove us back to the airport so I could drop Ana back off. Everything seemed pretty normal when she left. She hugged me tight and thanked me for taking her around and introducing her to all my friends, and she even promised she'd stay away from dudes when she got back to Oceanside.

As we stood there waving 'bye to each other outside the security check, I had no idea in the next six months things would turn so bad for my little sis.

My bus pulls into the little Greyhound terminal in Oceanside, and my aunt Reina and her new husband, Willy, are waiting there for me in their forest green station wagon. Me and Reina say our hellos and hug, and I shake Willy's hand, and then they take me directly to their church.

"This is real, Chico," Reina says, as we pass through the giant doors and into the dimly lit cathedral. Other people are walking in, too, smiling and hugging and making small talk. We pass this one crazy-looking dude in a long robe who waves at Reina and gives me a military salute. I salute him back, figuring he's loopy or something, but Willy tells me he's the head minister. We sit down in a middle pew, and Reina immediately turns my face so we make eye contact. "This is what you need right now, Chico. Not just you but *everybody*. Things happen in this life. Things we can't explain or understand."

I nod. And it isn't just Reina pushing me. Ever since this thing with Ana, I've wanted something real, too. Something I can hold on to. I look around at all the seemingly happy faces and think: *Maybe the answers are right here. Inside this church?*

A big woman climbs the stairs and sits herself at the organ. She holds her hands over the keys for a few long seconds, going for a dramatic effect, and then plays the first chord. Everybody springs out of their seats and starts singing and clapping their hands, swaying back and forth with the rhythm. My aunt gives me a songbook with the words, and I do my best to keep up. The big woman at the organ sings through a huge smile. She pounds the keys, occasionally looking over her shoulder at the crowd. The bald man in front of us pumps his fist and yells "Hallelujah!" at the end of every verse—just like they do on TV. During the second-to-last song Willy gets his new wedding ring stuck in Reina's hair. Everyone continues singing and clapping as she pulls and pulls to get herself free. But she's stuck. Willy acts fast, takes out a little pocketknife, and saws through the chunk of thick brown strands. Soon as she's free, a few people around us cheer and Reina does a little bow and Willy puts his hands in the air and says: "Everybody's okay over here. We're good."

After he says that, a few people around us laugh and then go back to their singing and clapping and swaying. But I can't stop staring at the small, uneven chunk cut out of my aunt's hair. It makes me feel incredibly sad. So sad I actually get a lump in my throat and feel tears pushing at the backs of my eyes. First time since my old man left me and my moms and my sis three years ago. The feeling only lasts a few short seconds, and then it's gone. But this thing I said that messed up Ana—I realize being here isn't gonna fix it.

"Didn't you just love it?" Aunt Reina asks me on the way home. She turns all the way around to look at me from the front seat. Reina's still pretty, especially when you consider she's got two daughters over eighteen and three grandchildren. Willy is white and has a sad little excuse for a ponytail. He drives with both hands on the wheel.

"It was pretty cool," I say. "Thanks for taking me."

Reina grabs my hand and squeezes. "Chico, you have to face what's happening with Ana through prayer. The fact is she's lost her way, and the only thing—"

"Oh, Reina," Willy interrupts. "Do you have to bring that up right this second? The poor kid just got here. You already dragged him to church."

"For your information, Will, I'm trying to explain my nephew that he's got an outlet."

"But come on, Reina. He doesn't need—"

"Listen, Will," she shoots back, "I think Chico understands what I'm saying." She turns to face me again, puts on a smile. "You do, don't you, Chico? Understand what I'm saying?"

I'm not home with my moms for thirty minutes when Medium's cab pulls into the apartment complex parking lot and the driver honks, interrupting our talk. My moms gets this stern look on her face and points at me. "Ana's gonna be okay, Chico. I'm not letting anything happen to my daughter. Now drop it and go. Everybody wants to see you."

I shrug, and she walks me to the door. "But when's she coming—"

"She's gonna be okay, Chico," she interrupts, and closes the door on me.

Outside, me and Medium wave at each other, and then she hugs me and tells the cabdriver: "Next stop, mister, is the state correction facility in Otay Mesa."

A couple months ago my uncle Rico was sentenced to eighteen months in prison for assault with a deadly weapon.

According to my moms, some guy in an Escalade cut him off on the freeway and Rico lost it. He waved the dude to the shoulder and then went off on his SUV with a sledgehammer. When the guy finally got out to fight, Rico dropped the hammer and beat the dude up so bad, he put him to the hospital.

"I been tellin' that man he gotta check himself," Medium says on the cab ride. "Told him a hundred times he better do somethin' with that temper 'fore he gets in *real* trouble. But do he listen to me, Chico? Uh-uh. *Now* look what he got his self into." Medium is my uncle Rico's long-term girlfriend. She's a light-skinned black woman with a voice that sits nice in your ear.

She says a few more things about Rico's temper, and then we both go quiet for a while. She stares out the right back window and I stare out the left. I meet eyes with a little pigtail girl sitting in the backseat of a fancy BMW at the last red light before we're there. She can't be more than six years old. Her blond hair is shiny and tied up in two black ribbons. The dad's in a suit at the wheel, sipping coffee. The mom's brushing out her long blond hair and saying something to the dad.

The girl smiles and shows me her doll.

I get a weird feeling in my chest and nod.

Inside the visiting room we sit in chairs separated from Uncle Rico by thick glass. Rico puts his fist up to the glass on his side, and I match it on mine. He looks thinner. And his hair seems different, shorter maybe. There are a couple grays in his goatee. Medium lets me have the phone first.

"What up, big Cheek?" Rico says. "I didn't do it!"

He laughs after he says that and looks at Medium, who is looking down at her hands. "Nah, for real, though. What up with that college you at?"

"It's pretty good," I say.

"And I hear you turnin' nineteen, tomorrow, that right?"

"Yeah."

"That's what's up, Cheek. Yo, when I was nineteen I had me about four or five honeys, boy. Had me a little pitchin' rotation, right?" He looks at Medium again, turns back to me. "Alls I'm sayin' is you better be handlin' your business up there with them educated honeys. Someone's gotta pick up the slack long as they got me locked up."

Medium takes the phone and cups a hand around the mouthpiece. I back up to give them room. They whisper to each other. They speak with their eyes through the glass. At one point Medium lowers the phone and covers her face with her hands, cries without sound. I try not to look. After a few more minutes she taps me on the shoulder and hands me the phone, says: "He wants to talk to you again."

I sit in front of my uncle and put the phone to my ear. "What's up, Uncle Rico?"

"You been to see your sis yet?"

I shake my head. "Nah, the place is all the way out in Arizona."

He nods. "Your moms gonna be all right? I heard she ain't talkin' to nobody about it."

"She swears everything's gonna be okay."

"You watch her for me, all right?"

"Yeah."

Medium pulls a tissue from her bag and dabs at her eyes. She takes out a tiny hand mirror, checks it, puts it back.

"Look, Cheek," my uncle says, leaning forward in his chair. "I maybe got things mixed up, but here's the way I see shit. Everybody takes a wrong turn at some point, right? *Everybody.* Your sis just went down the road a ways on hers. But alls I'm sayin' is this: If she do make it out in the end, finds her way back and makes it to be a grownup, I guarantee she'll be an interesting goddamn person. Which is a hell of a lot more than you can say about most people."

That night I'm roped into dinner at Aunt Sandy's apartment in San Ysidro, right near the border. My moms says it isn't that hard to spend a couple hours with the people who love you. And she's right. But as our bus cruises toward Mexico, I think I might rather do a hundred full-court sprints after practice than deal with Aunt Sandy's hysteria. "Why's she cry all the time, though?" I ask, as our bus lurches forward and stops, lurches forward and stops.

My moms continues knitting the first stages of a green and white blanket she's making for Ana and doesn't bother to look up. "She's had a tough life, *mijo,*" she says. "I don't think she can help it." She searches for something in her sewing bag, and when she can't find it she goes back to the blanket.

"But still," I say. "She just cries for no reason."

Aunt Sandy and her truck-driver boyfriend, John, greet us at the door with big smiles and tight hugs, and then we all stand there at the door looking at each other. Sandy gives me a big smooch on the cheek. John tells me to flex so he can feel my muscle. Their dog barks nonstop and jumps on both me and my moms. "Down, Pepper," Aunt Sandy says, swatting him on the snout. "You get off them two right this second, you hear?" She turns to us, says: "I'm so sorry, guys. Pepper's been a little riled up today. I don't know what's gotten into him."

Pepper's a hyper cocker spaniel who makes their whole house smell like wet rug. As Sandy and John lead my moms to the couch in the living room, Pepper continues barking and jumping on me. When nobody's looking, I swing my right foot into his ribs. Not crazy hard, but enough to let him know I'm not his boy.

"So, how are you, Chico?" Aunt Sandy asks when I make it into the living room. Aunt Sandy's overweight, and her long brown hair is the thickest you'll ever see.

"I'm good," I say.

The TV flickers behind us without sound. John comes back from the kitchen with a bag of Cajun Chex Mix, pours the whole thing into a bowl. Aunt Sandy's the first to reach in for a handful.

"Chico had a great season in basketball," my moms blurts out. "The coaches all told me they love having him, and he's getting nothing but As and Bs in all his classes, and somehow he still finds time to call his mom twice a week. Don't you, *mijo?*"

Aunt Sandy claps both her knees with the palms of her hands and sits up straight. "Oh, I bet you're just so proud of this boy. Basketball star and still hittin' the books. Isn't it wonderful?"

My moms smiles big and wraps her arm around my shoulders. And right then it hits me: *This* is why I'm here. I would pretty much do anything for this person.

"Yeah, he's a pretty all right kid," she says, and lets me go.

John swallows a mouthful of Chex Mix and says: "So, what exactly you studying over there, Chico? Besides the babes, I mean."

Sandy takes another handful of Chex Mix.

"Psychology," I say.

"Good," he says. "Maybe you can tell mother here what her problems are." Sandy pops a Cajun pretzel in her mouth, slaps John's shoulder; and the two of them laugh and laugh and laugh. My moms sneaks me a little look that says, *You'll survive.*

After dinner Aunt Sandy pulls me into her bedroom while my moms is on the phone with the people in Arizona. It's a cramped room with a big bed right in the center. No matter which way you turn, you gotta deal with the bed. "Your mom tell you Enrique's been bringing these home for me?" she says, pointing to the movie posters that cover every inch of every wall.

"Actually, she did," I say, which is a lie. We both stare at the posters. Enrique's her oldest son. He works at a local movie theater. He's thirty-three years old and has never been with a girl. He's a nice-enough dude, but there's something off about him. He wears thick glasses and moans when he speaks. He collects action figures.

I'm scanning the credits of the most recent Spider-Man movie when Aunt Sandy taps me on the shoulder. "This is what I wanted to show you, Chico," she says, holding up a little homemade picture book with the title *Even Butterflies Get Moody Sometimes*. "Your sister made this for me when she was in sixth grade. I still have it after all these years."

I take the book and flip through the colorful pages. I actually remember her working on this at the kitchen table. She made one for all our relatives. She used to sit there for hours and hours thinking up the stories, coloring in her own drawings.

"Such a wonderful little artist," she says, tears gathering in her eyes. "So creative. It just breaks my heart."

Aunt Sandy takes the picture book back, studies it again, and then places it back on her dresser. "Chico?" she says. "I wanted to ask you this. Do you have any idea what got into her?"

I let my back rest against the wall as Sandy stares at me, waiting for my answer. I slip my hands into my pockets and shake my head. "I really don't, Aunt Sandy. I wish I did."

Her upper lip trembles, and she collapses onto her bed in a sitting position, starts sobbing into her hands. I stand there watching her body twitch, listening to her make those little hiccup sounds. "Why would such a sweet young girl wanna hurt herself like that?" she says through her hands. "I just don't understand what happened."

She pulls a tissue from the box on her nightstand and blows her nose. Pulls a couple more and wipes her eyes. She looks up at me, her mascara all over her face now. "Why, Chico? Why would such a beautiful young girl *do* that to her own body? She's so smart and creative. And pretty." Sandy stands up and wraps her arms around me. She rocks me back and forth. "I'm so sorry, Chico."

The whole room is quiet except for the occasional hiccup sound and the squeaking of the floorboards as we rock back and forth. "You're so strong, Chico," she says through new tears. "And you don't push an old lady away. You just let her go on and on about whatever she wants to. You don't look down on her."

She raises her head and looks at me again. "I'm so sorry," she says.

When my moms and I get home, we stay up late watching *Saturday Night Live* and talking about everything except Ana. So finally, during one of the commercial breaks, I just come out and say it: "All right, Ma, give it to me straight. Is Ana really gonna be okay? Or are you just saying that?"

She frowns and gives me this harsh stare, sits up straight. "Goddamn it, Chico. What'd I tell you? She's gonna be okay. I won't let nothing happen to my daughter. Now drop it, all right? Now!"

"All right," I say turning back to the TV.

We sit in silence for a while after she says all that. The guy doing the fake news on TV says some pretty funny things, but neither of us laughs. During the next commercial she clears her throat. "Besides," she says in a softer tone, "it's my son's birthday tomorrow. We should only be talking about happy things, all right?"

"All right," I say.

A little after midnight she makes a bed for me on the couch, and I fall sound asleep the second my head hits the pillow.

• • •

This morning Moms woke me up with a plate of blueberry pancakes. The top one had candles in it, and she somehow burned in the number 19. We ate together in front of the TV, and then she scooped up our plates and told me to hurry up and shower because people would start showing up at eleven o'clock. I hustled into the bathroom and showered and got dressed, and when I saw I had fifteen or so minutes to spare, I wandered into Ana's bedroom. And I guess I was sort of surprised that it looked just like she left it. My moms hadn't touched a thing.

At first I rifled through her drawers, looking for clues. What would make my little sis, who was already thin and super pretty, almost starve herself to death? To the point that her body became so thin, my cousins said her clothes, even the smallest stuff she owned, hung from her shoulders and hips like a hobo. To the point that she lost so much of the hair on her head, she started wearing a wig. To the point that her bones went so brittle, she broke an arm just climbing the fence behind our apartment. To the point that one of her kidneys failed and she could hardly get out of bed. To the point that a doctor told my moms Ana would actually die if she lost even five more pounds, and said her only chance was if she went to this special in-patient treatment place in Arizona. Even found her a sponsor to help with the cost.

But the problem was, I couldn't *find* any clues. Not one. Everything seemed like the stuff you'd find in any normal girl's room. I got frustrated thinking maybe I just didn't know what I was looking for, so I plopped myself on her unmade bed to think.

And that's exactly where I am now. Sitting on Ana's bed with my arms crossed, looking around her room. Soon the doorbell will start ringing and the people in my family will walk in carrying a Tupperware thing full of marinated carne asada or chile Colorado, or they'll have a twelve-pack of beer or charcoal for the grill or a bottle of tequila. They'll all pat me on the back and hug me, and tell me: "Happy birthday, Chico." My uncle Ferni might try to give me nineteen punches in the arm. Reina's daughters, Veronica and Sofía, will bring their kids, and everybody'll comment on how big they've gotten. Uncle Rico will call us on the phone and tell us how much he wishes he could be here. My gramma will almost cry, explaining how she knows her Rico will turn his life around just as soon as he gets out. And when Aunt Sandy sees her mom all sad like that, she'll immediately begin to sob.

I stand up, walk over to the closet, and look in. Same stuff you'd find in any other girl's closet. I run through that one question she asked me back in my dorm room, when she came to visit. "What do these girls up here gotta do for you to really like 'em?" And my stupid-ass answer. "Be a perfect ten." I turn to look at the rest of her room again, run through that conversation again and again, the way I have a hundred times since my moms first told me about Ana on the phone. "What do these girls gotta do for you to really like 'em?" "Be a perfect ten."

The worst part is that I always try and think about what I'd say if I could do the conversation over. But I never come up with the right answer. Everything seems fake. Or too preachy. Or too honest. I try again as I study all the normal stuff my sis has left behind. Blank CDs and posters of The White Stripes. Notebooks slung around the room. Unfinished art projects. All of the things my moms has left alone. Painted lunch boxes. A magic kit. School textbooks. Piles of dirty shirts and jeans.

When I can't think of anything, I get pissed off and fling open the door to leave the room, and I damn near trip over my moms. She's sitting to the side of Ana's bedroom door, against the wall, holding her face in her hands and crying.

"Ma!" I shout. "What's the matter?"

She looks up at me with tears streaming down her face. "I'm scared my baby's gonna die."

My stomach drops, and I feel tears coming, too. But I manage to fight 'em off.

"I'm scared, Chico."

I sit next to her, put my hand on her shoulder.

"I'm so scared."

I try real hard to think about what I could say, but nothing comes at first. Just like when I replay my conversation with Ana. My head is totally empty.

Finally I blurt out: "She's gonna be okay, Ma!"

She looks up at me, her face a mess of tears.

"She's gonna be okay. I promise."

She nods and puts her face back in her hands and cries some more. And I just sit with her there, against the wall outside Ana's room, rubbing her shoulder.

Sweet 16 Plus

Wendy McClure

When I was eleven going on twelve, my mom gave me a copy of *The Woman Doctor's Diet for Teen-Age Girls*. She'd seen it on a sale table at Brentano's and had picked it up. "Not that I think you really *need* it," she said as she handed it to me. She just seemed to know that I would like it.

I did. I freaking loved it. It had a glossy jacket with the title in hot pink letters; underneath, the cloth cover was pink. And it was just for *teenage girls!* It was like getting my first box of tampons, except better, since I didn't have to actually bleed or anything in order to earn it. It was definitely a milestone— a sign that I was headed somewhere good (hello, *teen*ville), and for once, it was okay that I was "ahead."

For years I'd been considered big for my age. When I was ten, seventh-grade girls with spiky mascara would catch me with their stares as I'd walk by, because I was tall enough to look them in the eye. I felt like a mistake. But I was told that girls in my family shoot up in height early and then stop; at some point, soon, I'd no longer tower over everyone else. I liked that idea, that there was supposed to be an age at which time and all the other bodies around me would fall into sync. I imagined it would be like a cool movie called *We're All Fourteen*—maybe I wouldn't be the star, but at least I'd belong in the story.

It's true that eventually I wasn't the tallest girl anymore. But it sort of didn't matter, because I'd stayed the heaviest girl. Somehow, being fat meant I was never quite the same age as anyone else. Certainly I was young enough for grandmas and great-aunts to wonder aloud about the second helping I took. Or they'd ask me if I wanted to grow up fat like my mom, and I'd have to act young and dumb enough to just shake my head *no* and try to swallow the idiot logic of *not wanting*. My mom owned *The Woman Doctor's Diet for Women*; also *The Complete Scarsdale Medical Diet* and *The Pritkin Principle*. Obviously, she didn't want to be fat either.

What thrilled me the most about *The Woman Doctor's Diet for Teen-Age Girls* was not the possibility of losing weight but the notion that I could be a *Dieting Teen*. I saw myself at the threshold of an age when my body would make sense, and even better, I could get there early. I took the book up to my room and got on with my future.

I had a great time reading about the cravings that I, as a Dieting Teen, would soon have, also the binges, the slip-ups, the disastrous crash diets I might fall prey to. "Now, then, having nothing but juice for a whole week before the homecoming dance isn't the *best* idea, is it?" said The Woman Doctor. "Unfortunately, Karen learned the hard way." I wouldn't. I would learn it all—how The Pill puts pounds on, how dates blow diets; I even learned about something called *munchies*. "Those of you who've had the occasional marijuana cigarette at a party are no doubt familiar with this little problem," The Woman Doctor said. When I first read that part, I had the impulse to hide the book under my bed, but then I realized I didn't have to.

It was the eighties, when the hottest thing that you could wear was an artfully ripped sweatshirt that slipped off one shoulder. When I was in junior high, everyone's moms freaked out about those shirts—they exposed at least one bra strap, and we weren't old enough to dress that sexy. But by the time I reached my teens, "dressing older" had become a lot less sexy. The clothes I saw in *Seventeen* and *YM* rarely went above a size 12, so in order to find stuff that fit me, I *had* to dress like I was older—older as in "middle-aged."

The Juniors' section at Carson's had neon lights in zigzags on the walls. There were TVs set into the walls, and they'd play music videos, and it was stupid, totally stupid, except when they'd play that one by The Cure with all the socks, though obviously the store picked it because the socks went so well with the color scheme of the Juniors' department. God. But stuff in Junior sizes didn't fit me anyway, even though I was fourteen.

It wasn't so bad in the Misses' department, where clothes went up to a size 16. I could deal with being a *miss*. A *near* miss—I could shop within earshot of the Juniors' music and within sight of the videos. At best, shopping in Misses' was like raiding the closet of the big sister I never had. If I wanted a miniskirt or jeans, Sister Missy could usually provide. But there were also times when I suspected she was kind of a loser. She liked those sweatshirts with the polo collars. From what I could tell, she'd never aspired to go to art school the way I did; or if she *had* gone, it was a distant memory, and now she had this nice office job, and wasn't that easier, after all, to just give up? I tried to ignore those kinds of thoughts along with the embroidered sweater vests.

What was left of my reckless youth in Misses' ran out quickly, because the size 16s did, too. When I was fifteen, my mom pointed out that I'd have an easier time finding clothes in Women's World. "Women's World" was the store's euphemism for plus sizes. The *women* part let you know you were far from Juniors and Misses; *world* meant the distance was light-years away. "Let's just *look,* okay?" my mom said when she took me there. It was true that size 16s were everywhere in Women's World. So were sequined Mother of the Bride dresses. "You could wear *this* to the dance," my mom would suggest, holding one up. "Couldn't you?"

I did have some choices. If wearing "career coordinates" to school didn't appeal to me—like, for some reason—I could wear earth-motherly jumpers with whimsical patch pockets. Or I could wear billowy diva blouses with tiger-stripe prints. Or I could put my eye out with the hanger.

But I learned to adapt. I decided some of the big shirts and the baggy pants could *maybe* look *sort of* artsy. Exotic, even. With a little creativity, perhaps, I could assemble sophisticated-yet-fun outfits that flowed around me; I'd transcend age, *that's* how cool I'd be. I would be a Mysterious She floating through the mall, the school hallways, wherever, a cloud of rayon and intrigue. People would whisper, "How old is she, this enigmatic woman-child?" and I'd catch their eyes with a wise look that said, *Ah, but do not ask such things.*

This look did not wind up working as well as I'd hoped. I was in tenth grade and sometimes looked like Bea Arthur. Really. It got so I would check out the clothes on the TV show *Golden Girls* and think, "Huh, I could work with that."

And then one day I was on my own in Women's World: I was sixteen. I was a bad girl far from home. Or else maybe I'd been on my own for years and years. Or I was just some fat girl buying old-lady clothes. I wasn't sure. I'd just taken my mom's credit card, and I didn't know what that meant. It was the Carson's charge, and I'd swiped it from her wallet; I'd figured that a few extra charges on her bill would go unnoticed if they were from the department where she shopped. This was just the sort of stupid shit that sixteen-year-olds tried sometimes, I thought. I didn't know that for sure, but if I got busted, it could be my excuse.

I wandered around the racks. I tried on a long white shirt that I didn't especially like, but it would do. At the counter, one saleslady folded the shirt while the other rang up the purchase. When I handed over the card, I tried to meet their eyes. I wondered if they'd take me for a woman, fully of age, shopping in the plus size department. I wondered if it all looked enough like my life that I wouldn't get caught at it.

It wouldn't be the worst thing to get caught. The little printer inside the cash register whirred. I didn't know what would happen, just that whatever happened would be the truth.

And then the saleslady handed me the charge slip and I had to sign it. "Thank you for shopping Women's World at Carson's," said the saleslady. "Come back again."

I went home and stuffed the Carson's bag under my bed. And then later I pulled it out and laid the shirt on my bed; I took the tags off with scissors. I hadn't thought at all about whether I wanted the shirt. I ripped out the stupid shoulder pads; I hacked off the collar. I would try to make it into something I could live with.

Some Girls Are Bigger Than Others

Sarra Manning

It was meant to be a summer full of boys. The ones who worked at the funfair on the pier, their tans deepening as the weather got hotter and they took off their T-shirts to spin squealing, sunburned kids on the Waltzers. The packs of guys down for the weekend to our dreary little seaside town, who wanted to steal kisses behind the arcade. And the boys from school who suddenly got taller and fitter and knew how to look at you like you were the only girl in the world.

Which was why me and Jules had got summer jobs at the ice-cream parlor on the pier. Before my dad left, we used to spend two weeks in Majorca, so my parents could hurl insults at each other in a Mediterranean setting. But now money was tight, and if I had to spend summer at home, then I needed to be where the boy action was. And when we turned up the first day in our matching white short shorts, the owner, Big Don, increased our pay to £5.50 an hour and all the sprinkles we could eat.

Yeah, it was going to be the best summer ever. And then three things screwed it completely and utterly up. Jules got appendicitis and was rushed to the hospital. Her parents were so relieved that she didn't die that they took her off to Fuente Vera, in Spain, to convalesce. And Jules asked Louise to go with her because I'd insisted her stomach pain was trapped wind. Also I look way better in a bikini than her.

Then it started to rain. And never stopped, so the skies were permanently dark and the sea was an angry, bubbling gray cauldron. Big Don wasn't too bothered that his only customers were geriatrics making a small vanilla cone last an hour while they waited for the rain to die down to a light drizzle, but I was devastated at the lack of cute boys coming in.

Then the summer went from sucking to officially sucking like no summer had ever sucked before. Because one morning there was Rosie cowering under the parlor's jaunty awning when I arrived to open up. "Oh, hi, I'm Rosie," she whispered, so quietly I could barely hear her over the relentless drip drip of the rain.

"Cath," I said, giving the door a hard shove because it tended to stick. She was looking at me funny, because we'd been at junior high together, but Rosie'd gone on to the posh girls' school and she was wearing mum jeans and it seemed easier to pretend that I didn't know her.

She was still the same quiet Rosie who crept around the edges. She looked around the ice-cream parlor nervously as if she expected the metal scoops to suddenly spring to life and start attacking her. I opened the storage cupboard and grabbed a handful of yellow cotton. "Here, put this on," I ordered. "Loo's over there."

Rosie reached out to catch her regulation I SCREAM, YOU SCREAM, WE ALL SCREAM FOR ICE CREAM T-shirt, and I realized that she had changed. I mean, she was still small and round, and her messy, mousy hair still obscured her pink cheeks, but Rosie *had* grown up. Or at least her breasts had. They were *huge*. And when she emerged from the bathroom in the figure-hugging T-shirt, her tits entered the room half an hour before she did. It was so very unfair, because my own boobs were no more than an afterthought. Large breasts were wasted on a girl like Rosie.

"It's a little bit tight," she bleated forlornly, staring down at her chest in dismay.

"Yeah, sucks to be you." She'd bogarted all the breast-age, so no way was she getting any sympathy from me. Then I launched into her orientation. "It's pretty easy to figure out, apart from when someone wants to build their own sundae," I explained at the end, and Rosie nodded and waited at the counter eagerly, like we were about to be besieged by hungry customers.

Surprisingly, we settled into a comfortable routine over the next few days. I'd serve if a hot guy came in, but the pickings were pretty slim and I always got the mint choc chip and the pistachio mixed up. Rosie had way more patience at dealing with people, and when it wasn't raining, she actually volunteered to hand out flyers, because she was a loser.

But mostly I sat reading magazines and Rosie sat reading books. Proper books like for school, with tiny letters and fugly paintings on the front of girls who looked all swirly and watery.

We didn't talk at all. Until the day the guy who worked at the face-painting booth came in for a sundae. I rushed to serve him because he was under fifty and passably fit apart from the whole geek chic thing with his hipster specs and Jack Purcells and, oh my God, a bloody cardigan, but Rosie was already brandishing one of the scoops purposefully.

I watched in amazement as he took the Build Your Own Sundae promotion to scary places that it was never meant to go. The chocolate ice cream, double chocolate ice cream, chocolate fudge ice cream with chocolate sauce was against all laws of God and Weight Watchers.

"I saw you handing out leaflets this morning," he remarked to Rosie, who blushed more furiously than usual. Boys probably didn't talk to her that much, except to comment on her mammoth appendages. "I could take some for the face-painting booth if you wanted."

Rosie did want. She wanted so badly that she even gave him an extra helping of chocolate sauce.

"Do you fancy him?" I asked when he'd left with his sundae perched precariously in one hand as he shifted the box of leaflets under his other arm.

"I fancy not handing out leaflets in a sudden downpour," Rosie muttered. Her voice dropped. "'sides, boys like that don't fancy girls like me."

"What, dorky boys in cardigans?"

"Whippet-thin arty boys with a casual insouciance," Rosie said, which seemed like brainiac speak for dork. It also seemed like we'd used up our allotted word quota for the day.

I soon realized that Rosie really didn't like me. Like, she would never speak to me about anything not ice cream–related. She'd either bury her head in one of her boring books or willingly serve customers without waiting for them to cough pointedly first.

I tried everything. I asked her about music, but she only liked whiny emo bands. I asked her about her favorite TV shows, but she was a freak who didn't have her own TV. By the time I asked her what her favorite color was, I was officially desperate, but she just mumbled, "Green," as Cardigan Boy walked in.

I'd given up trying to serve him because he always waited until he caught Rosie's eye, but she was steadfastly gazing at the syrup bottles until I gave her a theatrical nudge. "I don't serve dorks, so he's all yours," I drawled.

I could tell that Rosie didn't know whether to glare or drool. Instead she blushed and gestured at the assembled ice creams. "Well?"

If I'd been Rosie, I'd have engaged in some flirty talk involving the word "vanilla," but Rosie just waited until Cardigan Boy decided on a praline and peanut butter combo. She dropped the first scoop on the floor, and because I'm a saint, I offered to mop it up while she tried again. Her legs were totally shaking, and when I finally straightened up, it was in time to hear him say, "Nice pin," as Rosie handed him his change.

The door had barely had time to close behind him before she burst into tears.

Rosie wouldn't say why she was crying. She just ran into the loo. When she came out, her eyes were as pink as the rest of her face, like she'd been scrubbing at them with the scratchy toilet tissue that Big Don got from the cash-and-carry instead of the posh stuff we had at home.

"Are you all right?" I asked, in the hope that she'd unburden, but Rosie simply sniffed a bit and picked up her book.

It was much, much later, when I'd just locked up and was gazing at the bulging sky and waiting for the first fat drops of rain to start plopping down, that Rosie spoke.

"I thought he was different," she said, trying to yank the zipper of her windbreaker over her breasts. "But he's the same as all the other boys."

"He is different from other boys. He wears a cardigan, for God's sakes."

"No, I mean it was just about these, wasn't it?" She gestured at her chest. "He wasn't looking at my pin at all."

I looked at her pin, which was hard because her breasts really were attention hoggers. READING IS SEXY, it proclaimed, which it *so* isn't—but if Cardigan Boy really had been looking at her pin and thought it was cool, then they were, like, kindred spirits or something.

"Maybe he was looking at your pin but your boobs are in the same area so he had to look at them, too. They are kinda . . ."

"Big?" Rosie suggested coldly. "Ginormous, don't get many of them to the pound, could have someone's eye out—whatever you were about to say, don't bother. I've heard it all before."

"I was going to say gazeworthy," I snapped, because she could just get over herself. Lots of people would pay good money for a pair that weren't even half as impressive. Just a sweet little set of 34Cs, f'rinstance. "How big are you, anyway?" I heard myself asking. "Like 40DD?"

"Oh, piss off," Rosie hissed in a very un-Rosie-like manner and stomped off.

"I was only asking," I pointed out, following her because I wanted to get off the pier before the heavens unleashed. "Boys like boobs—deal with it." Which was precisely why I had a pair of rubber chicken fillets stuffed into my bra cups.

"Well, I like boys who can see beyond my chest to the person underneath," Rosie muttered. "If he doesn't like me for my personality, then he's not worth it."

"You want to know something?" I asked her, and didn't wait to be told no. "You are a *moron*. Cardigan Boy obviously fancies you and you fancy him. I don't think your tits have anything to do with it."

"They're called breasts, actually," Rosie snarled, and getting her to drop the mousy act was the most fun I'd had in weeks. And maybe getting her and Cardigan Boy together would be fun, too. Or not fun exactly, but it was always raining and I hadn't had a chance to go anywhere near the pier's funfair, and God, I'd never been more bored in my tender young life.

"Do you want to know what your problem is, Rosie?"

"Apart from the way you keep haranguing me with

rhetorical questions?" She folded her arms over the offending areas. "What is my problem, O wise one?"

"You think everything is about your breasts; but they wouldn't be so noticeable if you stopped tugging at your clothes and drawing attention to them every five seconds." Rosie's hair was in her face, and I couldn't tell whether my words were having any effect. "You don't make the best of yourself. You should do something with your hair and stop letting your mum buy your clothes."

"She doesn't buy my clothes—"

"Well, it looks like she does." I tried to soften my voice, because we were getting off topic. "Look, Rosie, you might read lots of books, but they're not teaching you important boy-getting life skills. Twenty-five percent of your problem is obviously low self-esteem, and the other seventy-five percent of your problem will disappear if you let me work on wardrobe, grooming, and getting you a bra that actually fits."

Rosie took the bait at last. "What's wrong with my bra?"

I came right out with it. "You have a monoboob. There's meant to be two of them, not one long sausagy thing hanging there. I'm not a lezzie or anything, Rosie, but I'd really love to know what's going on under your clothes."

I hadn't even finished my sentence before Rosie bolted across the road and narrowly avoided getting mowed down by a bus.

And that was that. If Rosie wanted to spend the rest of her life being a monoboobed freak, it was nothing to do with me.

But three days later, after Big Don had been in to give us our wages, Rosie sidled up as I stacked my magazines in a neat pile. "It's late-night closing, isn't it? Will you help me buy some new bras?"

Rosie had a long list of acceptable behavior for our bra-buying expedition. She refused to have her boobs measured. I wasn't allowed in the changing room. The words "knockers," "bristols," "norks," and all other variants were banned, and I wasn't to speculate on what her size might be.

I agreed to everything, because even walking to the main shopping drag together was a big thing for Rosie. Acceptance was the first step to recovery, blah blah blah. And I almost shed a tear as I saw the light dawn on Rosie's face as I extolled the virtues of underwire bras and she snatched a handful and hurried to try them on. She was actually figuring out the basic rules of girl stuff before my very eyes.

When Rosie reappeared, and headed toward the cash register with her hands full of new bras and one graying old one, she was walking very oddly, as if her center of gravity had totally shifted. Maybe it had, because her boobs were no longer one weird roll propped on her chest, but like actual proper breasts. They were still enormous, but at least they didn't look like they should have their own national anthem anymore.

"You have a waist now," I told her in amazement after she'd paid. "You look super fierce." I expected Rosie to give me another speech about how she only wanted to be judged for her lame personality, but a tiny, pleased smile played around her lips.

"I'm having this major epiphany," Rosie confessed. "I

always thought it was superficial to care too much about clothes and hair and it was the inner me that counted. But maybe the outer me should look more like the inner me."

She really needed to come with subtitles. "What does the inner you look like?" I asked.

Turned out that Rosie's inner me looked like the girls in the books she read: quirky and mysterious, which I translated as a muted color palette and lots of V-necks and wrap tops to minimize her mammaries. We trawled through Top Shop and H&M, and Rosie tried on everything I suggested. It was like having my own life-size Barbie doll.

"Everywhere's shutting," Rosie protested when the security guard locked the door behind us as we left the last shop. "You haven't bought anything. I thought you'd blow your wages in an instant."

Which just went to show that I had more layers than anyone ever gave me credit for. "I'm saving up for something," I said vaguely.

"College?" Yeah, like that would ever happen.

I waved an airy hand around. "Well, let's just say that I have plans to invest in my future." And saving up for breast enlargement so I could snare a premier division footballer/pop star/actor/clubowner and never have to work for a living was a totally valid career option. But I wasn't going to tell Rosie that.

Every day the skies got darker and the rain got more biblical and we'd camp out in one of the booths so I could impart all the wisdom I'd acquired in my sixteen years.

Rosie took notes on why a green-based foundation

would tone down her red cheeks and the difference between a pear shape and an hourglass figure. And when I
was done imparting, she made me laugh by inventing this
whole other life for Big Don where he ordered girlfriends
off the Internet. She was dead sarcastic and funny once you
got to know her.

There were hardly ever any customers, but when
Cardigan Boy came in, Rosie would hide from view and
whisper, "You serve him, Cath, please."

But on Thursday when the bell above the door jangled,
I'd just given my nails their second coat of The Lady Is a
Tramp, so with a long-suffering sigh, Rosie hauled herself up.

"Hey, I haven't seen you for ages," he said, and she almost tripped over her feet.

Then his eyes widened at new improved Rosie in a
black V-neck sweater that fitted properly with a little felt
corsage pinned to her shoulder and a pair of jeans that
didn't give her a mum bum. And game on, because Cardigan Boy was looking at Rosie in exactly the same way that
he'd looked at his tropical fruits sundae. Mind you, he'd
looked at her like that premakeover, too.

"I hope this doesn't sound sketchy, but I've got something for you," he said nervously, reaching into the inner
depths of his jacket while Rosie looked intrigued but
nervous, because Cardigan Boy was coming over all stalk-
ery. "I saw you reading *Bonjour Tristesse* the other day; then
I found this in a charity shop and you've probably already
got it, but the cover's really cool."

He pulled out a moldy paperback, its pages tinged yellow. Rosie took it and turned it over carefully like it was

some holy relic, as I squinted over her shoulder to see the book title: *For Esmé—with Love & Squalor*. Whatever. But Rosie's face lit up, and in that split second she was so beautiful that it made me blink rapidly until she looked like she usually did.

"That's so weird—this is on my to-buy list," she said. "And I love old editions of books. If I really like the book, it makes me kinda sad that someone gave it away. Do you know what I mean?"

Cardigan Boy knew exactly what she meant. "I have this hardback of *The Portable Dorothy Parker* from the 1940s that I found in Cancer Research. Why would anyone get rid of that?"

It was all very well bonding over books, but they still weren't getting the basics sorted. Not unless I did it for them. "I'm Cath, this is Rosie, and you are . . . ?"

"David," Cardigan Boy said. "Never Dave or Davy or Id."

And Rosie totally laughed even though it was the lamest joke I'd ever heard. It was adorable in the dorkiest, geekiest way possible.

How was I going to get Rosie and David away from ice cream and on an actual date? I needed to get in their heads and try to fathom out the geek mindset, but God, that was so hard. Then on Tuesday Rosie was banging on about her latest boring book while I was flicking through the local paper, and I had such a genius idea that I almost fell headfirst into the strawberry ice cream that I'd left out on the counter to soften.

When David finally came in, I elbowed Rosie out of

the way so I could get to him first. We went through the usual sundae business while he cast longing glances in Rosie's direction; then I moved in for the kill.

"Hey, have you ever read *The Great Gatsby*?" It was a perfectly natural question for me to ask, so there was no need for him to smirk.

"It's one of my favorite books," he replied, and Rosie opened her mouth to start wordgasming about it, too, but I rustled the paper as a diversionary tactic.

"You know they made a film of it, right? It's playing at the Rep Cinema tonight." Rosie went very still, like she knew exactly where this was going and she wasn't too happy about it.

"I've always wanted to see it," David enthused, walking into the clever trap I'd set and making himself right at home.

"Really?" I smiled sweetly at Rosie, whose eyes were promising a little light torture. "Rosie's dying to see it, too, but she hasn't got anyone to go with. I refuse to watch any film that wasn't made this century."

If David paused for longer than five seconds, I was going to brain him with a box of sugar cones, but he was already turning to Rosie with a casual smile that I knew masked the fear of rejection. "You probably already have plans, but if you fancy going with me . . . ?" He trailed off and stared down at his Jack Purcells.

Which was just as well, because Rosie was doing a good impression of a slack-jawed yokel. "Um, if you don't mind, I guess that would be, er, like, all right," she muttered.

"No, I don't mind. If you're sure you don't . . ."

It was like watching some nature show on the Discovery channel about the mating habits of geeks. Watching two bears clawing each other into bloody shreds would have been less painful. "Jesus!" I snapped, pushing his sundae at him. "Come and pick her up after work. Six sharp so you've got time to get the tickets. Now go away. We might have some other customers in a minute."

As soon as he was out of the door, Rosie turned on me furiously. "You're absolutely unbelievable, Cath," she began, her face flushing. "You pimped me! He was obviously just being polite because you forced him into—"

"You're welcome," I said when she had to pause for oxygen. "If I were you, I'd start doing your makeup, because you're still crap at applying liquid eyeliner."

"He paid extra for the superior comfort seats," Rosie told me the next day as we shivered behind the counter. It wasn't actually that cold, but the rain was thudding against the window and it felt like we should shiver. "And then we shared a tub of popcorn and he squeezed my arm in a really sad part of the movie, but it wasn't in a lecherous way. It was a very empathetic squeeze."

"And then what happened?" I prompted, eyes wide.

"We went for coffee and talked about the movie and F. Scott Fitzgerald's other books and loads of things, and then he walked me home," Rosie finished with a smile that was verging on smug.

"And did he kiss you? Like, with tongues?" It came to something when I had to get my vicarious snogging thrills from Rosie.

"Maybe he did, maybe he didn't," she said coyly. "But I'm seeing him tonight. We're going to a gig. You should come," she offered, because Rosie was a sweet but totally naive girl who thought it was polite to invite friends along on dates.

"Nah, you're okay." I shrugged. "The music you like hurts when you listen to it."

"Some of David's friends are going to be there." Rosie's face squinched up. "Maybe they won't like me. They're all at university or art school, and they'll think that I'm fat—"

"You are not fat," I interrupted angrily, because at least she didn't go straight up and down like me. "You're curvy. Big diff. And you're really smart and funny and you should stop judging yourself on what you think you look like. It's so pathetic. And don't you forget it."

Rosie didn't forget it. Maybe that's why she was a big hit with David's friends. She even went bowling with them later in the week, then turned up for work in this old-fashioned dress that hugged her curves like she'd just stepped down from one of those 1950s pinup-girl pictures. Her boobs were still mighty, but it was like she'd grown into them. "David's friend Kara gave me this," she said, twirling so I could see how the circle skirt foofed out. "She said I had the perfect figure for vintage clothes."

I was happy for her. Really I was. That's why I folded my arms and pouted. "You could get something in H&M that's practically identical," I noted savagely. "And no one would have died in it."

Rosie just twirled a bit more. "We're going to hang out at David's place tonight," she said dreamily. "He's cat-sitting for his parents, and you have to come, because I've told everybody about you and they want to meet you."

I had better things to do than hang out with a bunch of students. Well, normally I did, but Jules was still in Spain and everyone else was on holiday and I couldn't take another night of my mum ranting about my dad. "What have you told them about me?" I asked suspiciously. "That I thought *The Bell Jar* was about chemistry?"

Rosie rolled her eyes and gave me a little pat on the hand. "No, I told them that I was finally figuring out how to be the girl that I always wanted to be and it was all down to you."

It was my turn to blush, because I never got compliments like that. I got comments on how shiny my hair was or how I was really working my short shorts, but no one ever commented on my, like, inside stuff. "Whatever," I drawled to hide my embarrassment. "Okay, I guess. Like, how bad can it be?"

It was bad. A world of total bad with added bits of badness. I walked in and was confronted by six full-of-themselves students who looked at me and decided instantly that I wasn't worth knowing. Actually they didn't even look at me. They looked at my legs in my denim miniskirt and my padded boobs in a tight pink shirt and my shiny, lightened hair, and that was enough.

Rosie kept shooting me these anxious looks, so I plastered on my brightest smile and let the conversation about carbon footprints float right over my head. She belonged here and I didn't. In fact, I could feel Rosie slipping further away from me every time one of David's friends popped into the parlor to say hello and Rosie would smile and joke with them instead of hiding behind her hair.

We still hung out at work, but it wasn't the same. Rosie was kicking it freestyle these days, and now that I had nothing left to teach her, there wasn't really a lot to talk about.

So it was a huge relief when it stopped raining and the sun came out. Big Don dragged the Mr. Whippy machine outside to take advantage of the day-trippers, and I volunteered to run it. I couldn't quite master the necessary twirling action, but I really needed to start on my tan and scope out the talent.

The sunshine had made the boys emerge from wherever they'd been hiding, and I remembered what summer was meant to be about. And I had to get my focus on. I'd lost too much time for sticky kisses and holding hands with out-of-towners. I needed to think about who'd still be around in September, when everyone at school was bragging about Pedro the cabana boy and François the deck chair salesman. If I had a boy in the bank, so to speak, rather than living off memories, then I wouldn't need any sympathetic looks because newly one-parent families couldn't afford luxuries like package holidays to Corfu.

First I considered Jimmy from the Waltzers because he was really fit, but he had dirty fingernails and everyone knew he'd done really gross stuff under the pier with a girl from the doughnut stall. Loz from the Ghost Train always winked at me when he came to beg for change, but he had a zitty back and he spent the off-season in a spliff haze. I needed a boy who was way more thrusting and dynamic.

Eventually I settled on Kieran from the bumper cars, because he played football for the local club's youth team, he drove a black Jeep, and when he sauntered bare-chested along the pier with a cocky smile, his muscles rippled and it was like having a religious vision. He was perfect for me.

I pulled out every single weapon in my arsenal. I went two shades lighter on the blond scale, fashioned my T-shirt into a bandeau to show more skin, and smiled flirtatiously every time he walked past. Nothing seemed to work, and the skanks from the café opposite had set up a tea stall outside the front door and weren't above whistling at him. I could have been invisible for all the notice Kieran took of me

Summer was limping to a halt and I could feel the weight of going back to school already crushing down on me. I needed a Plan B on the boy front, I thought as I served up cone after cone. And as soon as I thought it, a voice in my ear roughly enquired, "You all right, then?"

It was Kieran. I mean, of course it was Kieran, and all of him was twinkling at me: his eyes, his smile, the bleached tips of his spiky hair. I stuck out my chest and fluttered my eyelashes. "Yeah," I said, staring at his mouth. "You all right?"

"You're Cath, right?" Kieran asked, and I forgot the impatient queue of customers and the girls from the café trying to kill me with their collective dirty looks. Because Kieran was all there was, and his eyes were running up my legs, over my tummy, lingering slightly at the boobs, then coming to rest on my mouth as I poked my tongue slightly between my lips like I was deep in thought. "Yeah," I said after about five seconds. "And you're Kieran. Your cousin knows my mate, Jules."

"So, like, do you want to go to the Pier Summer Party with me on Friday?" I had to stop myself from squealing, because we were so *on*. Every summer the business owners who rented space on the pier held a party for their underpaid, overworked summer staff. It was at some cheesy club in town, but it was just about the most exciting event of the season. And Kieran wanted to walk in with me in full view of those jealous ho bags from the café who'd taken to shouting rude remarks at me in their quiet periods. Result!

"Sure, that sounds cool," I said casually as Kieran asked for my number. And it was that easy to get the guy you fancied—if you weren't Rosie.

I was in torment most of Friday as I tried to dish up ice cream and beautify myself. There was a hairy moment when I spilled a glob of body shimmer in the chocolate chip, but I smooshed it around with a scoop, and I don't think anyone noticed. Well, only Rosie, and she didn't count.

Once we'd finally closed and I was carefully applying glittery eye shadow, I saw her sulky reflection in my compact. "Rosie, you are going to this party, right?" I asked suddenly, because I hadn't thought to check.

"Why would I willingly spend time in a room full of people I'd normally cross the road to avoid?" Rosie said, though a simple "no" would have done. "It's not my scene."

"But you have to come!" I yelped, closing my compact with a snap and fiddling with the neckline of my dress so it didn't dip down low enough to reveal my darkest secrets. "Is David going?"

"It's not his scene either." Rosie sniffed, like they were too good to get down and dance to songs that had an actual tune. "Anyway, you're going with Kieran, so what's the problem?"

How could Rosie not know this stuff? "Because I don't want him to think I'm some friendless loser who spends the entire night clinging to him," I all but wailed. "Look, just come for a couple of hours."

"I can't," Rosie said firmly. I'd preferred her when she'd been a total pushover and had no social life to interfere with my plans. "We're going to see a band and we have to catch a train and—"

"God, I can't believe you're one of those girls who dump their mate as soon as you get a boyfriend," I burst out. "You wouldn't even have hooked up with him if it hadn't been for me."

"That's not fair," Rosie protested, her voice throbbing like she was getting teary. But she was still picking up her bag like she intended to abandon me. "That's a really unkind thing to say, Cath."

I was about to say a lot more really unkind things when there was a tap on the window, and I whirled around to see Kieran raise a hand and shoot me one of those wolfish smiles, which made my knees shake. "Oh, why don't you just go home and read one of your moldy books," I hissed. "That's the closest you'll ever come to having a life."

"I can't believe that I actually thought you were my friend," Rosie choked out as she hurried to the door and almost knocked Kieran off his feet. And he could take his eyes off her tits, too.

"We were never friends," I stated clearly. "I just felt sorry for you." And before Rosie could put a complete damper on the evening, and to get Kieran's attention away from her scene-stealing mammaries, I dragged him down for a long, tonguey kiss until she was just a fat, round blob in the distance.

The party was fantastic. When I walked in with Kieran, everyone turned to look at us like we were this golden couple or something. I kept a tight hold of Kieran's hand, and maybe it was that and the kiss we'd had before that made him so, like, demonstrative.

"You're so hot, Cath," he kept saying, while rubbing his hand against whatever part of my body was nearest. "You're the sexiest girl here."

Technically I wasn't, because Lizzie who worked on the rock stall had got through to the semifinals of this TV modeling competition, but whatever. Kieran was totally acting like we were officially dating and kept the Bacardi Breezers coming. And he only let me leave his side to go to the loo, where I adjusted the fillets and applied more body shimmer to give me the illusion of cleavage. When I got back to the bar, Kieran was hemmed in on all sides by those cows from the café. I staggered over so I could simultaneously wrap myself around Kieran and shoot death stares at them.

The party was winding down by then, and Kieran and I ended up on a sofa at the back of the upstairs bar. Normally I don't like getting off with someone in public, but it was dark and there wasn't much to see—just Kieran sprawled out on top of me while he tried to hump my leg. It reminded me of the fight between my mum and dad when she'd taken the dog to the vet to have his balls chopped off. The dog, not my dad. And I was so busy thinking about castration and poor old Muttley that I wasn't paying any attention to where Kieran's hands were going, which was straight into my bra cups.

"What the hell is that?" he muttered in my ear, and before I could process the full horror of the moment, he'd yanked out one of my rubber fillets and was staring at it in bemusement.

"'S nothing!"

I tried to make a grab for it, but Kieran was already jackknifing off the sofa so he could look down and see one breast all perky and firm while on the other side there was nothing but gaping material, and he laughed. He actually laughed. "Are you really a girl, Cath, or are you just a bloke in a dress?"

"Give it back!" I squealed, trying to make a lunge for him, but he took a hasty step back, and I fell off the sofa and landed in a heap on the floor. Which would have been Kieran's cue to apologize, scoop me up in his arms, and kiss me better.

He didn't. Kieran just gave the chicken fillet a tentative prod and sniggered again. "I heard you were tight, and now I know why."

Okay, Kieran wasn't the most sensitive specimen that boykind had to offer, but I've always had a weakness for the rugged bad boys. So I should have known what would happen as Kieran's pack of bumper-car mates tripped up the stairs. "Look what Cath was packing under her dress," he shouted as he threw the fillet at them.

I cried the whole way home. And then my mum wanted to know what had happened, and when I told her she said that all men were bastards; then *she* started to cry, which made me cry even harder. Then I cried because I'd ripped my new Zara dress and I missed my dad and there was no one to say that it would be all right because nothing was going to be all right ever again. Not until I got my new boobs and I met some rich guy who'd take me away from this stinking town and everyone in it and I never had to come back.

In fact, I spent most of the night crying when I wasn't throwing up, and the next morning I really wanted to call in sick. But I had a new appreciation for my £5.50 an hour and the bigger boobs it would buy me, so I stuck on my fake Gucci shades and my longest skirt, which just skimmed my knees, and staggered to work.

Rosie was already waiting for me to open up, and I just couldn't deal with her right then. Especially as the first words out of her mouth were, "You were vile last night."

"Don't talk to me," I spat, and tried to ignore the way her face sort of collapsed in on itself. It was raining again, which suited me just fine because sunny skies would have made my head hurt even worse, so I sat at the counter and proceeded to ignore Rosie. By some sheer feat of inner strength that I didn't know I possessed, I managed not to cry for a few hours. Not even when some cow started moaning about the chocolate chip ice cream tasting funny.

I scooped and assembled cones and asked people if they wanted "sprinkles or sauce?" in a dronelike voice.

I just needed to last until six and then I could go home and go to bed and cry a bit more, but time had slowed down to a crawl and there were still two hours until I could herd the last ice cream guzzlers out of the shop. I stared at the clock on my phone, then gave a little start as it beeped. Then I gave an even bigger start when I saw that I had a text from Kieran.

It was a bit late to apologize but *at least* he was apologizing. That was something. I eagerly opened the message, and then I really did burst into tears and six o'clock be damned. Once I started crying, I couldn't stop and was only dimly aware of someone guiding me into the storeroom, where they sat me down and tried to dab at my face with a damp tissue.

It took a long while for the sobs to die down to hiccups, and Rosie was still crouched down in front of me with a concerned expression on her face.

"What about the shop?" I spluttered.

Rosie shrugged carelessly. "I put the 'back in five minutes' sign up on the door about half an hour ago," she said breezily, as if Big Don's profit margins weren't her problem. "Is this about Kieran? What's he done?"

I tried to explain what had happened, but every time I opened my mouth, a fresh volley of sobs emerged. In the end I handed over my phone so she could see the picture of my rubber fillet stuck to a wall and the text: "Feel like chicken tonight? Call Cath on 077557 . . ."

She gave a little gasp, stared fleetingly at my chest, which was as flat as my mood, and then narrowed her eyes. "I knew he was no good," Rosie announced. "You can't trust a boy who bleaches his hair. It shows a lack of character."

It was such a Rosie thing to say that I actually smiled. Until I looked at my phone and my face crumpled again. "I bet he's sent it to everyone in his address book and they'll have sent it to everyone in their address book." I hunched over as the enormity of the situation dawned on me. "I'm going to be a flat-chested freak of a laughingstock. Oh God, it will be all round school, too. This must be how Paris Hilton felt when her sex tape got leaked."

There was nothing else to say, so I decided to start crying again.

She totally didn't have to, but Rosie was really cool about it. She let me skulk in the storeroom so I could come up with a convincing argument to persuade my mum to get a bank loan so I could have my surgery before I went back to school. Then I could pretend that the rubber fillets weren't mine and also start a vicious rumor that Kieran wore a codpiece. It was a long shot, but it might just work.

My musings were interrupted by a knock on the storeroom door, which burst open to reveal Kieran standing there, Rosie's hand round his wrist in a vicelike grip if the ouchy expression on Kieran's face was anything to go by.

"I can take it from here," she called out, and over her shoulder I saw David and a couple of face-painting-booth geeks fade into the distance. "Kieran has something he wants to say to you," Rosie told me in a singsong voice, and I couldn't understand why Kieran was letting her treat him like a bitch until she did something with her nails and his wrist that made him yelp like the spineless wanker that he really and truly was.

I lifted up my blotchy face and wished that I still had my shades on. "What could you possibly want to say to me?" I asked dully.

"I'm sorry," he spat sullenly.

"Why don't we try that once again with more feeling?" Rosie suggested pleasantly. "Like we discussed after David threw your phone off the end of the pier or I'm digging my nails in again and I don't care if it is your throwing arm."

"I'm sorry that I acted like a Nean . . . like a Nean-der . . . like a tool last night. It was really disrespectful of me to treat you so objectively, and . . ." Kieran faltered and Rosie hissed something in his ear. "I need to appreciate women for their minds and not just their individual physical attributes." He broke off from the script to shoot me a reproachful look. "I was only having a laugh, Cath. Why you being so touchy about it?"

"Because you humiliated me in front of all your friends," I snarled. "And I bet you sent that text to everyone on the south coast, and now I'm going to have to be home-schooled or something."

Rosie let go of Kieran, who rubbed the back of his hand and flushed. "Actually I ran out of credit after I sent you that text," he admitted. "I didn't send it to no one else, I swear. And I don't mind that you've got no tits—I still fancy you."

The huge wave of relief swept away everything else in its path. But if there was a footballer in my future who'd lead me by the hand to a world where I was special and important and there was a never-ending supply of designer handbags and spa memberships, it wasn't Kieran. "Well, I don't fancy you," I confessed flatly. "Not anymore. Not after what you did."

He stumbled out after that, mumbling something indistinct, though the word "bitch" was loud and clear and Rosie raised her eyebrows at me and sort of shrugged.

"Thanks," I said, even though it was really inadequate because she'd just saved my life.

But Rosie seemed to understand, because she gathered up my bag and shades. "Come on—let's get out of here," she said decisively. "You need junk food."

It wasn't until I was tucking into a huge basket of fries in the nearest pub that didn't ask for ID that Rosie remembered to text David to let him know I wasn't going to top myself or anything. I felt a pang of envy, because when would it be my turn to have a devoted boyfriend? "See, it's stuff like this whole Kieran business that is exactly why I've spent my summer dishing up foul-smelling ice cream so I can save to get my tits done," I blurted out before chugging down a whole glass of Diet Coke, because I was never drinking alcohol again, not even when I was eighteen and legally old enough.

Props to Rosie because she didn't chew me out for letting her rattle on about her own breast issues without ever 'fessing up. "Maybe it's not your tits that's the problem; maybe it's the guys you go for," she said mildly.

That was so typical of her! "I can't help it if I'm genetically programmed to only fancy boys who want the whole package; blond hair, long legs, big boobs."

"But you said it was all about confidence," Rosie pointed out, and she was starting to sound a little peeved. "That I should stop worrying about what other people thought of me."

"Well, maybe I kinda lied," I admitted. "Confidence only gets you through the door—doesn't get you into the VIP room, though."

Rosie threw her hands in the air like I was getting on her last nerve or something. "You know, if you used your powers for good, not evil, you could totally eradicate world hunger in six months," Rosie said, as she swiped one of my fries. "Seriously, Cath, don't you think if you stopped concentrating on making your hair super shiny and chatting up creepy boys, you could use all that determination to do anything you wanted?"

"But all I want is to have super-shiny hair and actual breasts so I can attract a really cute boy with lots of money who'll take me away from this shitty little place," I said around a mouthful of hot potato. "Ain't gonna happen any other way."

"Well, you could study hard, go to university and get a really well-paid job," Rosie suggested, but my face scrunched up because I was that close to crying again.

"That would take way too long," I moaned. "And I'd make an ace trophy girlfriend. . . ."

Rosie's eyebrows shot up so high that I thought she'd need surgery to remove them from her hairline. "You have to figure out who you really want to be, then make sure the people in your life are going to help you achieve that. Like you helped me see beyond my 36Fs."

It wasn't that simple but now I was distracted by Rosie's true bra size. 36F? F? How could such a thing be possible when I was a 32AA? Before I could ask Rosie, she was digging in her bag and pulling out a notebook and pen. "You need a proper plan for the future," she said firmly. "One that doesn't involve invasive surgery."

"You sound like my career advisor, except he thinks my only future is working in a call center," I grumbled.

Rosie ignored my whining and held her pen poised over a snowy white page. "You're very goal orientated and love a challenge, and we're going to come up with a project to make the most of that potential. Now, what do you really want to be when you grow up, and if you say footballer's wife, I'm going to smack you."

"We'll keep in touch," Rosie insisted on our last day, when we were helping Big Don out by eating our way through the last of the sugar cones. "I'm still going to need tons of fashion advice."

But we weren't and she wouldn't. Rosie had her own sense of style now, and she was doing a gazillion university applications and had plans to visit David in London. While I'd be stuck retaking the finals I'd spectacularly failed because it was hard to cram when your parents were throwing crockery at each other. Which was why I'd thrown her bullet-pointed list of my future goals and aspirations in the trash. And I was thinking about buying bigger boobs again, because finding a rich boyfriend seemed more doable than ever passing English.

"Yeah, for sure," I sighed, but Rosie didn't even notice my utter lack of conviction, because she was dragging out a huge brown paper parcel from the back of the storeroom.

"I prepared some audio-visual aids for your project," she said, thrusting it into my hands and smirking when I nearly collapsed under the weight. "No peeking until you get home."

When I got home, my mum was well into the first bottle of wine of the evening, so I carried the package upstairs and ripped into it. I sifted through the collection of CDs and yellowing books that smelled of damp until I found a note written in Rosie's crabbed scrawl.

Dear Cath,

Before I met you, these were the people who showed me that there's a whole big world out there and that who I am isn't who I'm always going to be. I hope they do the same for you.

Love, Rosie

It was really sweet of her, but I wasn't Rosie. We were completely different people. Like, the huge diff in our breast sizes wasn't a big-enough clue. I shoved the package to one side, and then Jules called me and I forgot about it.

I kept forgetting about it until one night in October, when there was nothing on TV and I'd just dumped another lad from the school football team because he spoke only in grunts. I groped about under the bed and pulled out the first book I could reach: *Madame Bovary* by some bloke called Gustave Flaubert.

I took a deep breath, turned to the first page, and began to read.

Tale of a Half-Pint
Margo Rabb

I was the shortest girl in my class every year since kinder-garten. It didn't bother me until everyone else began to develop miniskirt-worthy legs and tube-top-deserving chests, and I continued to resemble a cast member from *Romper Room*. In eighth grade I made the mistake of wear-ing overalls to school, an outfit that caused a classmate to comment: "Are you *five?*" In New York City, where I grew up, sneaking into clubs was the quintessential teenage rite of passage, but I knew I didn't even dare try; the bouncer would probably ask if I'd brought my sippy cup. I was eter-nally underweight despite eating well, and though skinny is the cultural ideal, skinny accompanied by buckteeth, braces, glasses, a chubby-cheeked face, and hair that frizzed like a poodle's was not a good thing. "When you're older, you'll be grateful for looking so young," my mother said encouragingly, but that was the problem—I was never going to grow older. Never.

I attempted to look mature by slathering on makeup and tottering in high-heeled shoes, which caused another friend to inform me, "You look like a little girl trying on your mother's clothes." My father was happy that I looked young, since it meant he could sneak me in for the twelve-and-under rate at the movies, which he did until I was twenty-one years old. At that point the lingering humiliation of his habit finally took its toll, and I yelled at him in the lobby of the Cineplex Odeon in Manhattan: "You can't do that anymore! I haven't been under twelve for *ten years!*" To which he shrugged and stated matter-of-factly, "It's three bucks, though."

In ninth grade my friends acquired fake IDs, went out dancing at Limelight and Nell's, and started dating. I still looked like I should be reading Archie comic books while I twirled the propeller beanie on my head. By my sophomore year of high school I still hadn't kissed a boy, and I was deeply convinced there was something wrong with me, some clear defect that made the guys not like me. The problem wasn't just reaching a peak of five feet tall (with heels on)—it was everything. My nose was too big. My hair was too thick. In fact I had a growing suspicion that I might be completely hideous and disgusting. What if no one ever found me attractive? There was a girl in our high school who had modeled for *Mademoiselle,* and when I ran into her on the subway one morning, I stared at her as if she were a rare gazelle in the zoo. What would it be like to have those long smooth legs, that sleek shiny hair, those clothes that looked effortlessly perfect, to be so unabashedly, clearly beautiful—to *know* that you were beautiful? What would it be like to have that confidence?

Then, when I was fifteen, my father, who'd had severe heart disease for many years, needed triple-bypass surgery. It wasn't certain whether he would survive. During his extended hospital stay I was called in to see my high school guidance counselor. We discussed my father's condition for two minutes, and then she folded her hands and proclaimed, "I think the real problem here is that you have anorexia."

I gaped at her. Anorexia was one thing that I definitely did not have. I later found out that nearly every time a thin girl entered her office, she diagnosed her with an eating disorder. At least it made me realize that things could be worse—I could actually *have* an eating disorder, on top of everything else. I never went back to her office again.

My father recovered from his surgery, but a few years later my mother was diagnosed with melanoma that had spread to her liver, and she died ten days after the diagnosis. Losing her, and my father's still uncertain health, shook me to my core. Her death stripped me bare, down to the essentials. I no longer had any patience for superficial things. Thoughts I used to have, such as *It's so horrible that my hair is frizzy,* seemed ridiculous to me now; for a long time, I didn't have the energy to care much about how I looked or how I was perceived. So I could never sneak into a bar—so what? Did it really matter? No, it didn't. It took too much effort to try to be someone I wasn't. My mom's death gave me perspective—long legs, sleek hair, and fashion-magazine clothes were not important things in the world.

Her death changed the way I thought of my body as well. I discovered a fear of it—I would sit in the bathtub inspecting the moles on my skin and wondering if I might die suddenly like she did. Other times I would sit in the tub hugging my limbs, thinking, *Thank God I'm healthy. I'm okay.* That sense of gratitude for being healthy has never left me. My body has its defects, is far from perfect, but I've never again taken for granted the fact that it works.

I'm grateful now that I was a late bloomer, that I was able to grow up slowly, that I had those extra years of childhood. I'm glad that I didn't have a serious boyfriend until I was in college, and though the things I did when I was fifteen (spending time with my parents and my sister, being with girlfriends, reading books, enjoying time alone) seemed nerdy and dorky, they were the things that made me who I am. The heroines in the books I read, such as Anne in *Anne of Green Gables,* Laura Ingalls Wilder (a.k.a. Half-Pint) in *Little House on the Prairie,* and Anne Frank of *Diary of a Young Girl,* weren't inspiring for their physical beauty but for who they were: smart, resourceful, strong girls. The time with these books, the time spent learning who I was, eventually gave me a sense of confidence—the elusive confidence I'd thought that gazelle-girl on the subway must be brimming with. In retrospect, I'm sure that she was just as insecure as everyone else. A sense of confidence can't come from other people telling you you're beautiful, or from what other people think of you at all. It can only come from yourself. One of my favorite books has always been *The Little Prince,* and in seventh grade I copied out *What is essential is invisible to the eye* onto my denim notebook binder—and finally, years later, I began to believe it.

Of course I wish I could say I followed that tenet implicitly always, and never again had doubts about my looks, but that wouldn't be true. Most recently, after giving birth to my daughter, my stomach really looks like a human being was living in there for nine months—and didn't exactly leave the place as she found it. In fact, it looks like she had a dance party in there, a rave with some crowd surfing and raising the roof. But that's okay—it was worth it.

And my mom was right after all—the older I get, the happier I am whenever I'm mistaken for being younger. Not long ago I went to the movies with my very tall husband and his equally tall sister. I was standing between them in my thick down hooded coat, looking like Kenny from *South Park,* and the ticket seller asked, "Two adults and one child?"

I didn't mind.

The Day Before Waterlily Arrived

Jaclyn Moriarty

The day before Waterlily arrived was the day Granny Smith tried to make a Sunday roast.

(Granny Smith. Harp, harp, harp.)

The Sunday roast was chicken. Granny Smith brought it to the table out the back. She was wearing the zip-up jacket with the hood.

She put the chicken on the table and both hands in the pockets of her jeans. She stood like that a moment, staring into space.

(Harp, harp, harp. Looks as if I'm trying to say that Granny Smith was always harping on. I'm not. She was not. Au contraire.)

We waited. She was quiet. I was starving.

(This was four o'clock.)

Markus was kneeling on the lawn. Pieces of his bicycle around him. I was sitting on the wooden bench, my knees up to my chin.

Granny Smith breathed. Her eyes flickered the table. I'd been setting that table the last hour. There were place mats, napkins, paper cups, drinking straws, side plates, and a basket of sliced white bread. There was a plastic jug of water, a couple of cans of Pepsi, a bottle of Kentucky bourbon.

I'd been thinking if I just kept setting, I'd kind of draw the chicken to the table.

Granny Smith was silent for so long, I forgot where I was. I started an imaginary argument in my head. It was with my history teacher. It went like this:

MS. WALCYNSKI: You want to avoid failing this course? Travel back in time, take a few photos, and staple them to your next assignment.

ME: You're joking, right?

> (Ms. Walcynski shakes her head.)

ME: That's *ridiculous!*

> (Other kids mill around. They look at us with interest.
> Ms. Walcynski shrugs.)

MS. WALCYNSKI: It's up to you, Kirsten. Fail if you prefer.

> (Now I'm getting mad.)

ME: Have you lost your mind? There's no such thing as time travel! You can't make passing a course dependent on doing something *physically impossible!*

MS. WALCYNSKI: Well, but I am!

> (She throws back her head and laughs.)

"Let's eat!" Granny Smith said suddenly.

And her hands jumped from her pockets clenched like fists.

Markus brushed the wrenches and bolts from his jeans. I put my feet down from the bench and relaxed my angry face. ("We'll talk about this later," I hissed at Ms. Walcynski. She just laughed again.)

The chicken was tied up with string. Markus and I raised our eyebrows at each other: *She knew you were supposed to do that?*

"Your brother will carve?" Granny Smith said to me.

I looked over at Markus.

"He will," Markus said.

(But Markus is not my brother. We're the exact same age, for a start. So how would that work?)

Granny Smith pulled the string loose from the chicken. The string looked like a shoelace. A chicken-greasy shoelace.

(Well, okay. We'd be twins. If he were my brother, we'd be twins. But he's not. We're not. Au contraire.)

Turned out it wasn't a shoelace. It was the pull string from Granny Smith's zip-up jacket.

"No, don't—" Markus and I both reached out to stop her. But too late. She was threading the chicken-soggy pull string back into her jacket.

Markus carved the chicken.

(We're not even related, Markus and I. If we were, I might be a genius like him. But we're not, I'm not, et cetera.)

Markus paused and scratched his chin with the knife. Because he's a genius, he can do this without drawing blood.

"This chicken," he said, "isn't cooked."

He pressed the knife hard against the golden chicken skin. He drew blood.

"It's raw actually," he murmured to himself.

I looked around for accompaniments, like potatoes or beans or even a little white porcelain gravy boat.

But this was it.

"I don't care," I said. "Give me some of that chicken."

Granny Smith kept right on threading the string into her jacket. "Bit of raw chicken never hurt a soul," she said in her wise voice.

Markus breathed slowly through his nose.

"Give me some," I said again, reaching for the chicken plate, but he slid it out of reach and shook his head.

"Kirsten," he said.

Now Granny Smith stood up, took the chicken on its plate, and stepped into the house. We listened. But it wasn't the creaking of an oven door we heard; it was the snap of her foot on the kitchen garbage bin and a heavy, heavy thud good-bye.

Markus tossed me a slice of white bread and grabbed a couple for himself. He jumped from the porch to the lawn, walked by the pieces of his bicycle, and headed down the back to the shed. That's where he keeps his special projects.

(Granny Smith is not our granny either. She's a foster carer named Magda Smith, and she's kind of old. She calls herself Granny Smith. Like the apples. It's her joke. Harp, harp, harp.)

The next day, Monday, Waterlily turned up at our school.

"Her name is *not* Waterlily," Bella Martin breathed.

But it was.

Mr. Hazel, our year advisor, said so. "Waterlily will take you for your first class every day this week," he said. "She'll be going through the homerooms one by one, and class 8C, you're the lucky first! A break from your regular schedule, eh? Enjoy!"

He grinned, but people gave him hostile looks.

"Why were we not informed about this?" Joshua Todd demanded.

"Yeah," everybody agreed.

Mr. Hazel's shoulders sagged. "You were," he told us sadly. "We sent those notes a few weeks back. Remember? Your parents gave permission. The special course?"

Everybody looked to Joshua Todd. He nodded, curtly, once.

"Oh, *yeah*," we all said now. "That's right."

We turned our smiles onto Waterlily and examined her attire.

Her clothes were long and thin. Her blouse was soft and see-through. She'd worn a slip underneath, with little shoestring straps, one of which was tilting to the right. The slip was turquoise. The blouse was pink. Its sleeves reached down to caress her long, thin fingers. Her fingernails were painted vibrant orange.

"Those colors don't match at all," Bella Martin breathed.

Waterlily heard this—her eyes seemed to change focus—she pulled her sleeves even farther down, curling in her nails, and wrapped her arms tight around her chest.

Mr. Hazel talked some more, but you could tell that his spirit was gone.

We'd snuffed it out.

You never know a teacher's breaking point. He left the room in a huddled, weary trudge.

We turned our stares on Waterlily's face. Her body seemed to falter, but she held it up by leaning against a desk.

"I'm here to learn about you," she said. She almost whispered, that's how soft her voice was. She had no skills of projection.

"*What* did she say?" Bella Martin breathed.

"She wants to learn about us," Markus answered clearly in his deep, throaty voice. My nonbrother Markus. His shoulders straightened. He gazed at Waterlily. The sun gazed through the window at his face.

That night I picked up Chinese takeaway. I got Steamed Dim Sum, Spring Rolls, and Deep Fried Duck. I was excited. But then, as I carried it home, the damp patches of oil crept through the bag and warmed my hand. So then I thought, *Oh, yeah,* and felt a bit depressed. My skin breaks out a lot these days. I keep forgetting, and buying fried food.

"You want to eat on the porch again?" I asked Granny Smith.

She was curled up on the couch watching TV. She didn't answer.

"It's a hot night," I told her.

She made a popping sound with her mouth.

I leaned out the back door to call Markus inside. He was cross-legged on the lawn.

"Where's your bike?" I said. "You sell it for a bag of magic beans?"

"Harp, harp, harp," said Markus.

(He says it low voiced, from the side of his mouth. I like the way he says it. Like a distracted seal. And another thing he says is: "Au contraire.")

"My bike?" he said. "I finished it." He stood up with a tiny smile. A flat metal object, the size of a bread board, in his hands.

"Watch," he said. He shook the metal object. There was a snapping, clicking, crackling, chinging, blinging—and his bicycle stood on the lawn!

I told you that Markus was a genius.

He'd invented a fold-up bicycle.

He folded it again. I followed him into the living room.

"Look," he said to Granny Smith. The same explosion of sound, and a bicycle stood in the living room!

She turned back to the television. Some nights she doesn't speak at all.

The next day, Tuesday, Waterlily walked into the classroom backward. She was swaying and stumbling slightly.

"She's inebriated," Joshua Todd said curtly.

But she was not. She was carrying a plastic children's sandbox. It looked like a sandbox to me, anyway. It had green scalloped edges. She was trying to tip it *ever so slightly* to get it through the door. People moved closer. She tripped quickly backward. People had to dive out of her way.

Someone was pushing the sandbox through the door.

It was Markus. He was helping her to carry it.

"Kirsten, can you clear those things off the front table there?" Waterlily asked me. "That's it, Sam—you help Markus with his end. Oh, Parthe, I'm so sorry I just trod on your toe! Ming and Daniel, stand clear or I'll do the same to you!"

The day before, she had asked us all our names. (Also our favorite Nintendo games, and bands and movies, websites and chemical compounds. So now she really knew us.)

People crowded close again, partly to see the sandbox. Partly to find out what she was up to with the names. Getting them all memorized so fast like that. Using them all in that high-speed, crowded way.

The sandbox sloshed quietly. It was full of water. Plastic bath toys floated merrily.

Nobody knew what to say.

That night I was doing homework. Anyway, some books were on the table and I was having an imaginary argument with my biology teacher, Mr. Carr.

Granny Smith was fast asleep in the doorway. She was propped against the doorframe. If there were an earthquake, she'd be all set.

"They haven't even got *astronauts* onto that planet!" I was telling Mr. Carr. "Have you lost your *mind?* How can you expect *me, a grade eight student,* to be up there on Venus collecting *samples* of *flora* and *fauna* for your class?!"

But before Mr. Carr got to explain himself, there was a sizzling, crackling noise from out the back.

Markus was standing on the lawn again, this time holding up a small green box about the size of a novel.

"You want to see?" he said.

He flicked his wrist—snapple, crickle, spark—and a green plastic sandbox sat on the lawn.

"You stole her sandbox?" I was impressed.

He didn't answer for a moment. He was looking at the sandbox. The dusk was gathering, and his face was deep in shadow. Eventually, he looked back up at me. "It's not a sandbox, it's a kids' wading pool."

"Okay."

He looked down awhile again and then remembered me. "No. I bought one like hers on the way home. This way she can keep it in her purse."

I tapped my foot. My foot tapping was crammed full of meaning.

But Markus had crouched down at the side of the sandbox and was talking to himself. "Adjustments," I heard him say. And: "Smaller than this."

The next day, Wednesday, Waterlily's sandbox was still on the table at the front. People weren't talking too much. They were sitting up on desks, looking at the sandbox with blank faces. *We're only looking at it,* our faces tried to say, *because it's right where our eyes happen to land.*

We were annoyed with Waterlily. It seemed to us that the sandbox—or maybe it was a kids' wading pool, like Markus said—either way, it was nothing but a cheap teacher's trick.

That parade of bringing it in the day before? After that, she *hadn't even mentioned it.*

She'd just spent the whole time telling us we're beautiful. All of us. Every single one. She hadn't got into the specifics of our beauty—that I might have liked—she'd just offered some general, sweeping praise. And then she said she knew we didn't believe her. She knew we watched TV and read magazines; she knew we were assaulted with images of perfection. . . . Here, to be honest, I stopped listening.

I tuned back in when I heard her voice slow down. She was telling us she knew something *else* about us. Enough, I thought, of your *knowledge*. But Waterlily was whispering for dramatic effect.

"I know," she said, "that each of you HATES at least one thing about yourself!"

(At "HATES," she really shouted, and everyone jumped, uneasy.)

Then the bell buzzed for the end of class, and we blinked and rubbed our eyes. And looked over her shoulder at the children's wading pool.

So this day, the next day, we assumed our glazed expressions. We were ready, on the defensive.

Except for Markus. He was all aspark with the suspense; his eyes leaped from the open door to the wading pool and back.

By the time she arrived, ten minutes late, people were talking stridently about the pointlessness of this class. "Shh," breathed Bella. "Waterbaby's here."

Waterlily hesitated just inside the door.

"It's not Waterbaby," Joshua said curtly. "Her name is Waternymph."

Here Waterlily seemed to take another step, just so she could hesitate again. If she'd been wearing a coat, she'd have slid one arm free just so she could stop with it halfway down her arm.

But this was summer. She was wearing something shimmering and sleeveless.

"Waternymph!" she said, and her beam switched onto Joshua. "I like that!" Her voice grew as she moved in toward us. "Maybe I'll change my name!" She seemed to think about this. She tilted her head in an engaging way, really considering.

An alarmed shuffle wafted around the room: *What? She'd change her name?*

Then there was a second wafting thought: *Wait. This must be another one of her attention-grabbing ploys.*

"But let me tell you," she said next (a smooth transition), "let me tell you why I chose my name."

Both her arms swung out toward her wading pool. "Come closer," she murmured. "Gather round."

We did. More quickly than we'd planned.

That pool was truly congested with colorful bath toys. They floated, placidly, in shallow water.

"See there?" She pointed to a toy. It looked like a scoop of mashed potato to me. Some flakes of pink potato skin on top.

"It's a water lily," Markus said.

Oh, yeah, everybody thought.

"This is a pond," murmured Waterlily. "And all these toys are the animals and plants of the pond. All these toys are *us.* The thing I *hate* about myself is this: I'm much too thin. I'm flat as a pancake. And being thin, I worry that I float on surfaces; that I never truly plunge the depths. But see the water lily? It's thin and it floats on surfaces, but it's *lovely.* See how lovely it is?"

No.

Not that plastic toy.

That wasn't lovely at all. It looked like mashed potato.

Still, we took her point.

"So that's me, I guess," she murmured, shifting toys around with her fingernails. "The water lily. That explains my name. Okay?"

So maybe she wouldn't change it after all.

People seemed relieved.

"You should see Larissa's painting," Joshua Todd said abruptly. He tilted his head at Larissa. "She did a painting of water lilies. It's excellent."

"You did?" Waterlily cried.

Larissa blushed. "It was just a study from the Monet painting."

"Ah," Waterlily smiled and turned back to the pool. Her nail found another toy. This one was clearly a flamingo.

"Larissa," she said, seeking out Larissa with her eyes. "You may be the flamingo. See how beautiful it is? See its peach-like blush? You're an enchanting girl to look at." This was true. Larissa is stupidly pretty. "But I know you hate the way you blush. How wrong it is to hate that thing about yourself! You turn the colors of a sunset! The colors of a flamingo!" Larissa blushed again.

Waterlily stood back from the pond.

"You're *beautiful*," she said to the room. "Embrace the beauty of the thing you *hate* about yourself."

There was a subtle shift in the atmosphere. Quiet admiration. She'd parried the attack on her name, *and* she'd explained her wading pool.

Sure, it was overkill. You didn't need a giant plastic toy to make her point. But when teachers try too hard, sometimes you forgive them.

That night Markus invented a fold-up easel with a set of paints and brushes. The size of a thimble.

Later, Granny Smith invited us to sit in the dining room. We looked around for food, but there wasn't any to be seen.

She took a handful of after-dinner mints from her pockets.

"Last things first," she said in her wise voice. We stared at her, and she laughed and laughed and laughed.

The next day, Thursday, I arrived at Waterlily's class in the middle of an argument with my drama teacher:

ME: *What* are you talking about?! I *can't* turn myself invisible! Have you lost your mind?! How can you—

But Waterlily, I noticed, was furrowing her brow.

There was a problem.

Joshua Todd had announced, curtly, that he couldn't miss algebra this morning. He'd have to skip Waterlily's class.

"And I can't miss wilderness studies," Bella added, breathlessly. "It's a *highly* important class."

"Do you even take wilderness studies?" Parthe demanded. "I've never seen you there."

"I don't think our school offers the subject," David

Fitz observed. "Wilderness studies? I've never heard of it."

Parthe said, "Well, but—"

Waterlily interrupted him. "I'm so sorry, Joshua and Bella." She sighed. "But Mr. Hazel was very firm. No exemptions allowed. If there were anything I could do, well, I would."

Then she talked some more about self-image and so forth. I got back to my arguments with teachers.

I tuned back in when she was standing by her wading pool again. People moved close to her, a bristling excitement. Who would be chosen for the next plastic toy?

(And would she distribute the toys at the end of the week?)

(No. We doubted it. She'd need them for her next class.)

At the pool she smiled shyly, then turned and leaned across the water. She was wearing bangles today, and a shortish dress. Her bangles clicked as she pushed the toys about. She was looking for something, frowning, her face turning pale pink.

"Here!" Gently, she flicked a plastic bird. Another flamingo? There was a breath of disappointment. Would she find a flamingo for each of us? But no, this bird was pale gray. It bobbed about a moment and then stilled.

"Bella," said Waterlily. But she kept looking at the plastic bird. "Bella, you are this heron here. I'm sure other people—people larger than you—are jealous of how slender you are. But I know you hate yourself for being too skinny. Just like me. Only different, too, because *my* thinness is just flat, whereas yours is all angles and bones. Much like the heron here."

We all looked at Bella, appraising her angles and bones. She was staring at Waterlily, concentrating hard.

"But the heron is streamlined, you see? Its shape is perfect for flying and for diving for its food."

"Okay," breathed Bella, still concentrating hard. I could tell she wanted to say, *But I don't fly or dive for food, so huh?* But she knew that would be missing the point.

"And here, see this fish?" Waterlily flipped another toy. It looked a bit like a shark, only there was something wrong with its face.

"It's called a paddlefish," Waterlily said, and now she straightened and fixed a gentle smile on Joshua Todd.

"Joshua," she said. "People turn to you for guidance because you're tall and handsome."

Joshua's eyebrows leaped. He seemed genuinely taken aback. Could he not have known that he's hot?

"You *hate* your nose," continued Waterlily.

Now Joshua's shoulders relaxed. He resumed his proud expression while everybody studied his nose. "It's a fine roman nose, but *you* think it's too long. You'd choose an aardvark for yourself if there was one here, I'll bet. But an aardvark is a creature of the desert. So. No. Here's the paddlefish—a gentle giant with a great big nose. There are different theories about why it has its long nose—something to do with electrosensory receptors . . ."

Her fingers trailed through the water.

"You're suggesting I have electrosensory receptors in my nose?" said Joshua curtly. Somehow he made the curtness ironic.

Everybody laughed. Waterlily looked up and smiled

with crinkled eyes. Markus's eyes, I noticed at that moment, crinkled in just the same way.

That night, Thursday night, Granny Smith was not at home. They called us from the club around midnight. It might sound strange, but those are happy times: Markus and me, walking the summer night streets, Granny Smith unconscious between us. It's like we've found a piece of junk on the sidewalk, and we've made the *crazy* decision to bring it home! Maybe we can knock it into shape somehow? Turn it into a piece of performance art? A cheap, broken piece of junk, light as an old broomstick.

She's just a pile of twigs, that Granny Smith. She's just an old used teabag.

Sometimes we talk.

"With some people," Markus said that night, "you think they're weak and soft, but they've got this hidden strength."

"Yeah," I said.

I thought he meant himself. He's a skinny little guy, and I figured maybe doing this was making him feel strong.

No need to tell him that all he was doing was carrying a used teabag.

"And they draw on their hidden strength to win," he said. "They triumph. In unexpected, almost insidious ways, in ways that are invisible to most, they win."

"Huh," I said.

No need to tell him I didn't have a clue what he was talking about.

● ● ●

Once we'd got Granny Smith through the door and tossed her on her bed, I thought we might share a plate of oven fries. But Markus said he had some work to do. He slipped back down the back.

He was up all night. I woke a few times and checked. Mostly there was the beam of a flashlight dancing in the shed, and the clinging, shuffling sparks of sound that meant he was folding things up. Once I woke to a *ca-clack, ca-clack,* coming from the living room. He was rolling Granny Smith's piano across the floor.

Another time I heard an engine start, and headlights slowly poured themselves into the backyard. He'd driven Granny Smith's car out of the garage.

I heard floorboards creak in my own room once, and a couple of times in Granny Smith's room, too.

I heard the squeal of bookshelves shifting across the floor.

Around dawn a tap turned on in the bathroom. Then, at last, the light went dim in his room.

I got up one more time. I stood in the quiet of his doorway and watched him in his bed. In the moonlight by his window: a fat green laundry bag.

Friday morning was Waterlily's last day with our class.

"Next week it's class 7B," she said. "I'm really going to miss you guys."

She talked about self-image some more. I was watching Markus. His laundry bag was at his feet. It was crammed with objects in various shapes and colors, some in the shape of tiny rolling pins, a few the size of decks of cards, some as small as lockets. There was a label affixed to each. Also, a larger label on the outside of the bag: *A Gift for Waterlily.*

I wondered if he'd be brave enough to give the bag to her. Or would he just leave it somewhere for her to find it? *She's just as shy as you are!* I sent him a thought message. *Don't be afraid!*

Then I remembered what he'd said last night, about soft, weak people having hidden strength. I realized he was talking about Waterlily. He was thinking of how she seemed soft and shy but she'd taken on Joshua and Bella the day before. He was hoping *he* was just like her, with hidden strength of his own.

Still, I thought, why give her that whole bag? The wading pool made sense. It was a sensible gift for her. But I knew for a fact that the laundry bag contained, among other things, a fold-up fridge full of food.

For all he knew, she might already *have* a fridge full of food.

(Also, what would Granny Smith think when she woke up from her hangover and found that almost every item in her house had disappeared?)

"Gather round," Waterlily murmured in her soft, blushing voice. We drifted to the wading pool one last time. "You've been waiting for this, haven't you? Probably haven't listened to a word I've said, waiting for this!" Now we all laughed loudly and happily.

"Parthe," she said, turning to Parthe's happy smile.

And then she chose pond creatures for us all.

"Parthe," she said. "You're the snapping turtle. You've

got such a long, thin, wrinkled neck. You hate your neck!"

It happened fast.

"Kylie, you're a dragonfly! You've got protruding eyes!"

She spoke in an excited, fluttering voice.

"Sam, you're a mosquito! That teeny head of yours!"

Her fingernail reached from toy to toy.

"Ming, your face is flat and squat—you're a leech!"

Her eyes darted between us.

"Daniel, *you've* got a drab and dreary droop—just like an owl!"

Her voice was warm as a heated towel. On it went, on and on. I can't remember everyone, but somehow they were all the same:

"Carlos, look at those bucky little teeth, my dear—you may be the beaver. Tatiana, you've got the big, soft body of an otter—whereas, Allie, now you're as shapeless as a tadpole! Chris, those beady eyes of yours are *exactly* like those of a muskrat. Abigail, you're a *big, fat slug!*"

Now she paused and smiled her pretty smile, hesitating. I sensed a curious shuffling sound around me—I think it was the sound of people's minds reconstructing themselves. The sound of people high-speed thinking: *She's not doing this to us, yes, she is, but I thought she was nice, no, she's not, there's a way out of this, no, there's not.*

"Markus," she said, sweetly. "Markus, your voice has that irritating croak. You may be the toad. And Kirsten." She turned to me.

"Kirsten." She smiled her crinkled smile.

There have been some scary times in my life, but I'm pretty sure this moment was the scariest.

Still, I straightened up and smiled right back.

"Kirsten," she said, "with all those pimples, you *must* accept the spotted salamander."

She stepped back from the wading pool.

I could hear a persistent yelping noise, but I'm not sure who was making it. Mostly there was silence.

I didn't know what to do with my face. I wanted to put it in my pocket, but how? My skin seemed suddenly alive with acne. (I'd been thinking it was clearing up a bit, to be honest.) Now I had to grip my hands together to stop them reaching up to scratch my face away.

"Well." Waterlily grinned. "Like I said, I'm going to miss you all!"

Nobody said a word. Nobody was sure what had just happened. Were we standing up and smiling at a teacher? Or were we drenched and broken on the floor?

"And I want you always, *always* to remember what you've learned about yourselves this week. Every single one of you is beautiful." She opened her hands as if to say: *It's as simple as that.*

In the quiet that followed, a TV image sprang into my mind: a crowd of people drowning, thrashing about underwater, but the camera cuts from their struggle to the picturesque stillness up above.

Now the bell was ringing.

Waterlily bit her lip.

People turned hesitantly, gathering their things. Nobody looked anybody else in the eye. People seemed to cower or limp along, trying to hide their faces behind hands, their bodies behind limbs, their bones behind skin.

Markus stepped toward Waterlily. "Do you need some help," he said, "moving this to the 7B homeroom for next week?"

Waterlily sighed with gratitude. "Would you, Markus? I have to move it at lunch time today. Could you meet me back here then? That would be *great*."

Markus nodded once. Then he turned and left the room.

His laundry bag was slung over his shoulder.

I was having an imaginary argument with myself.

"No," I was saying, patiently, "a genius does *not* become a moron overnight. That makes no sense."

But I was stubborn. "Sense has nothing to do with it," I replied, shrugging. "Markus has lost his mind. He saw what Waterlily's like, but he'd already fallen too hard."

"Impossible!" I rallied. "Maybe he just *said* he'd help her move the wading pool at lunch. And then he didn't show up!"

"No. Love is blind. And Markus never tells a lie."

This was at the end of the school day. I hadn't seen Markus since he left Waterlily's class that morning. I guessed he was probably hiding in a classroom with Waterlily somewhere, demonstrating all his fold-up tricks. She would be making gentle sounds of awe.

I was heading along the junior balcony. Feeling a little low.

"She was supposed to be here half an hour ago."

"Well, has anybody checked the message board? Maybe she left a note."

I slowed down without thinking. Those two lines had just slipped out of the Lower Staff Room door.

"Nope, no note here. Has anyone seen Waterlily around?"

Now I stopped completely. The grade 7 year advisor was just inside the doorway, calling out to the room, "Anyone? I'm supposed to be meeting her about her course next week."

"I was supposed to have lunch with her today," said another teacher's voice, "but she didn't show."

"She was going to take *me* through her course an hour ago," a third complained.

"Well, this is *strange*." The year advisor seemed suddenly excited; she was pivoting slowly on her heel.

Then her pivot turned her just enough to see me there. A horrified expression pounced onto her face, like a large, hairy spider: *A student is looking at me! Through the Staff Room door! What on earth?!* She closed the door abruptly.

I moved on, thoughtfully.

I walked toward the grade 7 classrooms.

Class 7B.

The door was closed.

I opened it.

Empty.

But there was Waterlily's wading pool on the table at the front.

So Markus *had* helped her bring it here.

I walked into the room. Had they spent the lunch hour chatting quietly here? Had she taken him into her arms and called him her darling little toad?

I ran my hands around the plastic of the wading pool. Or maybe it was a sandbox. Seriously, it could have been either. And touched a finger to the crowd of plastic toys. A couple bumped together, tilted, and straightened again. I couldn't find the spotted salamander, but there was the water lily now.

It still looked like a pile of mashed potato to me, with flakes of red potato skin on top.

And silver. There was a single flake of silver on top as well. The size of a silver coin.

That had not been there before.

"Hey," said a voice.

Markus was standing in the open classroom door. The laundry bag was still on his shoulder. "Walk home with me?"

We walked to the school gate and I turned left.

Then I realized I was walking alone. Markus had turned right. He was heading down the street toward a crowd of people waiting at the bus stop.

The crowd included kids from our class. Markus was tapping Larissa on the shoulder as I caught up.

"You are not a flamingo," he said to her, in his formal voice.

Larissa turned and stared at him.

He reached into his laundry bag and handed her a thimble. "This is an easel and some paintbrushes."

Joshua Todd and Bella Martin both turned around and looked. There was silence.

"No," said Bella, eventually. "It's a thimble."

"You have to shake it," I explained.

Markus kept his gaze on Larissa's face. "Your artistic talents make people happy. *That* says something about who you are." Larissa gazed at the thimble in the palm of her hand. Surprisingly, she did not blush.

"It's true," said Joshua. "Your paintings make me happy." (Now Larissa blushed.)

"And you," said Markus, turning to Joshua, "are not a paddlefish. Au contraire. This small purple pen cap is actually a large flashlight. Because you are a leader. A shining light."

Joshua put the pen cap behind his ear. "Thanks," he said curtly. I could tell that he was trying not to smile.

A gathering of people from our class had formed around us. They were looking at Markus's laundry bag but pretending not to look.

A bus was approaching. Markus reached into his bag and started moving faster.

"Bella," he said, "this is a box full of fireworks. You're lively and sparkling. Everyone likes to see you be your vibrant self." Bella looked surprised, but she held the tiny locket on her fingertip and studied it closely.

"Parthe," he said, "this might look like a fingernail but actually it's a bookshelf. Your mind is a remarkable collection of facts and entertainment."

"Kylie," he said, "these are binoculars. You are perceptive and see further into people's minds than most."

And so it went on. He gave out most of the things in his bag.

I should point out that his gifts were not exactly equitable. For instance, Sam got a whisk (he stirs things up when they need to be), whereas Ming got a car. It's true that Ming is great with machinery, but still. She now has Granny Smith's car in her back pocket.

Eventually, Markus stopped. Not everyone from our class was at the bus stop. "I'll give out the rest on Monday," he murmured, and then, to the group: "You should probably wait until you're home before you unfold them." Then he turned and walked away.

He didn't look back, but I did.

And what I saw was this: a kind of reshuffling. A smile was washing across the faces of the people in our class. They were gathering themselves together again.

We walked home together in silence. I wanted to tell Markus how proud I was of him. He kicked a pebble at me, with the side of his foot, and I kicked it straight back. So now he knew that I was proud. (I never kick pebbles around.) He smiled and started to talk as we turned into our street.

"After Waterlily's class," he said, "I went to an empty science lab. I worked on inventing a fold-up human being for a while. I just wanted to fold myself up. I felt like disappearing."

I knew exactly what he meant.

"But then I thought about Bella," he continued, "about how skinny she is—Waterlily was right when she said that Bella's nothing but angles and bones. But that's because she doesn't eat. She's *always* wanting to make herself disappear. I realized that Waterlily's view of us was warped. I realized that my laundry bag was better."

That made me laugh.

He realized that his laundry bag was better! Genius!

We were almost at our front door.

"I have to give you *your* gift, too," he said to me. "I was thinking of giving you the fridge. Because you like to eat. But this is the television. Because your mind is crowded with colorful pictures and words."

We could hear Granny Smith singing to herself inside. "Where are my things?" she sang. "Who took my things? Was it the pixies? Or elves?"

"Thanks," I said. "I guess I should unfold it and put it back, though."

"No rush." Markus sat on the edge of the front porch and swung his legs. I sat beside him.

Something was jiggling my mind.

"Markus," I said. "You said you went to the science lab after Waterlily's class, to work on inventing a *fold-up human being?*"

"That's right."

"And did you figure out how to do it?"

"Well," he said, "this morning I could only fold up a person to the size of a silver coin. But I've been working on it. And now I think I can do it even smaller."

He demonstrated. He was right.

"Before I fold *you* up," he promised, "I'll tell *you* how to unfold yourself."

We stayed out there for hours practicing. Now we can get ourselves to the size of small black dots. Markus said that whenever we want to travel, we can get into a postage stamp or onto the page of a book. And so we do. (Here we are now, actually:)

P.S.

One week later Waterlily still had not returned. The police came to the school. They interviewed our class. A few headed out to the teachers' parking lot and snapped some photographs of her car. Someone drained the water from her wading pool and carried out her toys in plastic bags.

●　●　●　●　●　●　●　●　●　●　●

HELLO my name is

Carolyn Mackler

Here's an occasional scenario in my life: I'm at a cocktail party, a work sort of thing for writers and editors and people in the publishing business. I've got one of those nametags stuck to my shirt, somewhere north of my chest and south of my collarbone. I'm clutching a perspiring glass of cranberry juice in one hand, and even though I probably should have mastered this skill by now, I can't figure out what to do with my other hand. I'm scanning the room for someone I know or, even better, a caterer with a tray of those vegetarian spring rolls. I keep seeing them circle the room, but for some reason the good food never comes my way. Finally I weave toward the buffet table, hoping to get my spare hand on a cube of Muenster cheese. But I'm suddenly intercepted by a random stranger who scans my nametag, looks me up and down, and says, "*Carolyn Mackler?* But you're not fat!"

I freeze. It's happened enough times that I should expect it. But I always freeze and my bony arm feels even more awkward dangling down my side and my cup feels so slippery I think I'm going to drop it and the glass will shatter and cranberry juice will splash all over my bony shins and bony ankles and bony feet. If people can have bony feet. I'm not quite sure about that.

Once I've thawed, the first thing I do is—and again, this baffles me—I smile. I smile and I laugh a little. I hate that I do this because I'd rather say, "Yes, I'm Carolyn, and if you please, DON'T TALK ABOUT MY BODY." But I smile because it's such a bizarre conversation opener and I was raised to smooth over bumpy moments, make everyone feel comfortable in my presence. And then, as the random stranger stares expectantly at me, I stammer and cough and then, well, I explain why I'm not fat.

Let me back up a little. I'm the author of a popular novel called *The Earth, My Butt, and Other Big Round Things*. It's about a plus-size fifteen-year-old girl named Virginia Shreves who is adrift in a family of skinny perfectionists. They work overtime to make Virginia feel like a chunky deadbeat who doesn't measure up. I don't want to give away the book, but ultimately Virginia realizes that they're wrong, she's cool, and she can be the star of her own story without having to starve herself.

Ever since the book's publication, I've gotten hundreds of letters and e-mails from teen girls. They tell me that *The Earth, My Butt, and Other Big Round Things* has made them stop hurting their bodies, quit their crash diets, get help for bulimia, find their way out of depression, and embrace themselves as they are. These letters are one of the most gratifying parts of my career, because no matter your body type, it's a minefield out there for American girls, and I'm honored to be a port in the so-called "storm."

But back to *Hey, Carolyn, you're not fat!* Let me just say here and now that I hate this moment. For one, it challenges my talent as a fiction writer, my ability to get inside someone's head and see the world through their eyes. I always want to respond with a quip about how J. K. Rowling wrote the Harry Potter books and she's not a boy *or* a wizard. And Dr. Seuss didn't eat green eggs and ham. And, no, sorry, Kate DiCamillo isn't really a mouse named Despereaux. Hate to break it to you.

But I never seem to go there. I'm always a little flushed because it feels like this person is *complimenting* me for not being fat. But I don't need those kinds of compliments, so I quickly launch into this speech about how I did so much research on Virginia, talked to friends who were curvy in their adolescence, read online rants from plus-size teens, and did tons of eavesdropping on buses and in Starbucks.

More than anything, though, Virginia's weight was a metaphor for all the ways we feel insecure, don't measure up, don't fit in, don't think we're as deserving as other people. Or I suppose I should say the ways *I've* felt insecure in my life. That's the therapy session I have to have with this random stranger at a cocktail party, when all I wanted to do was prowl the food table or gossip about celebrity melt-downs.

But here I am, telling this person about my teen years, about how even though I'm not plus size, there are so many ways in which I'm one hundred percent Virginia. I tell them how I grew up half Jewish in a small town where almost everyone else was Christian and how kids teased me about it in seventh grade, how some boys wore swastikas on Halloween and the teachers didn't do anything. I tell them how, even though I wasn't fat, I was tall and gangly and my nose didn't perk up like the other girls' noses. Every night in bed I used to push at the cartilage with my fingers. I tell them how I was flat chested, a total carpenter's dream, and used to supplement my mammaries with cotton balls until one day, at the mall, my brother revealed to everyone—including the guy I had a crush on—that I stuffed my bra. I tell them how I had scoliosis wore a thick plastic body brace, and in tenth grade a boy knocked-knocked on my stomach like I was a door.

Sometimes, if I'm on a roll, I say I had hard stuff going on at home. I don't describe how my brother hit me, and I definitely don't reveal the top-secret stuff, the things I don't feel comfortable writing about even now. But I often felt like the Dutch kid with my finger in the dike, keeping the water from crashing in. I could never share these things with my friends, though, and thus it always set me apart.

So that, random stranger, is how I got inside Virginia's head.

Oh, and there's this other part of that comment that

drives me crazy. Toward the end of *The Earth, My Butt, and Other Big Round Things,* when Virginia's dad tells her she's slimming down and in the past she would have happily lapped it up, this time she realizes she doesn't want him to discuss her body like it's the weather forecast. So she stares hard at him and says, "I have to tell you that I'd rather you don't talk about my body. It's just not yours to discuss."

That's how I feel, too. I don't want someone to assume my body is up for analysis. I don't want this outright acknowledgment that everyone is monitoring each other's weight, making judgments based on what they see. So maybe some people are thinking it? Well, keep it to yourself and let the rest of us go about our business.

The next time I'm at a cocktail party, I think I'll grab a Sharpie and scribble on my nametag: *Carolyn Mackler. Please don't talk about my body.*

This is probably a true story...

The Mating Habits of Whales

Barry Lyga

Illustrated by Jeff Dillon

I WAS TWELVE; SHE WAS TWELVE.

WE MET AT SUMMER CAMP THAT YEAR.

WE BOTH LOVED WORLD OF WARCRAFT.

GIRL *OR* BOY.

UM, HI. I'M DEVON.

MARJORIE.

...LEVELED UP AND USED MY SPELL...

REALLY? AWESOME...

SHE WAS THE SINGLE COOLEST PERSON I'D EVER MET.

WE SPENT A LOT OF TIME TOGETHER.

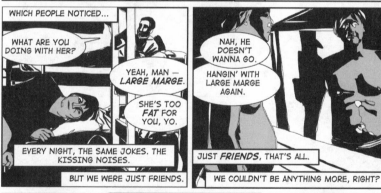

WHICH PEOPLE NOTICED...

WHAT ARE YOU DOING WITH HER?

YEAH, MAN — *LARGE MARGE*.

SHE'S TOO *FAT* FOR YOU, YO.

NAH, HE DOESN'T WANNA GO.

HANGIN' WITH LARGE MARGE AGAIN.

EVERY NIGHT, THE SAME JOKES. THE KISSING NOISES.

BUT WE WERE JUST FRIENDS.

JUST *FRIENDS*, THAT'S ALL.

WE COULDN'T BE ANYTHING MORE, RIGHT?

AND THEN, SUDDENLY, WE *WERE*.

125

SO I DID THE ONLY THING I *COULD* DO...

—GONNA SEE YOUR *GIRLFRIEND* TONIGHT?

NO.

AND SHE'S *NOT* MY GIRLFRIEND.

SHE'S JUST LARGE MARGE.

I DIDN'T SAY ANYTHING TO HER. THERE WAS NOTHING *TO* SAY, RIGHT?

I JUST STOPPED HANGING OUT WITH HER.

WHAT *ELSE* WAS I SUPPOSED TO DO?

I DIDN'T WANT TO HURT HER FEELINGS WITH THE *TRUTH*.

UH, NO, HE'S... NOT HERE...

I AVOIDED HER; TOLD MOM I DIDN'T WANT TO TALK TO HER..

SHE DIDN'T GIVE UP, THOUGH. EVEN WHEN I GOT HOME.

AND EVERYTHING WAS FINE.

FOR A WHILE.

Two years later.

First day of high school.

—WASSUP, BIG MAN?

—HEY, MAN—

I HADN'T THOUGHT ABOUT HER AT ALL. NOT SINCE THAT SUMMER.

HONESTLY, I NEVER THOUGHT I'D SEE HER AGAIN.

I COULDN'T STOP THINKING ABOUT HER.

MY DREAM GIRL WAS BACK. ONLY NOW...

AND I *ESPECIALLY* NEVER THOUGHT SHE'D BE...

YOU KNOW.

PERFECT. ABSOLUTELY PERFECT.

129

LOOKING IN THE MIRROR, I REALIZED: SHE DESERVED A BOYFRIEND WHO WAS SKINNY, LIKE HER.

I HAD TO MAKE MYSELF *PERFECT* FOR HER. AS PERFECT AS SHE WAS.

IT WASN'T EASY. I WORKED MY ASS OFF.

BUT NO MATTER WHAT I DID...

...NO MATTER HOW HARD I WORKED...

NOTHING.

I HAD A MISSION, THOUGH.

I HAD TO BE SKINNY.

I HAD TO BE PERFECT.

...NOTHING SEEMED TO CHANGE.

NOTHING.

WOW, LEFTOVERS...?

I GUESS I'LL, UH, TAKE IT TO WORK FOR LUNCH...

OK, DAD...

AND THEN ONE DAY, MONTHS LATER...

I FINALLY FIGURED I'D DONE ENOUGH, RIGHT? I WORKED SO *HARD*.

SHE HAD TO GIVE ME POINTS FOR *TRYING*.

I SAW HER BY HER LOCKER.

AND I WAS READY. READY TO *TALK* TO HER.

HEY, UH, MARJORIE?

SO, UH, I WAS WONDERING IF YOU MAYBE WANTED TO—

GOD, DEVON! BUY A FRIGGIN' CLUE, ALREADY!

BUT—!

I DON'T WANT TO TALK TO YOU.

LOOK WHAT I *DID* FOR YOU! CAN'T WE—?

HOW SHALLOW DO YOU THINK I AM?

I DIDN'T DISS YOU BECAUSE YOU WERE *FAT*.

132

It Is Good

Sara Zarr

The doctor had gray hair, wore a white coat and glasses, and didn't look like the type of man who had spent very much of his life smiling. I was sixteen and had been sick, feverish and achy with a bad sore throat. My mom figured I had strep. She sat on a chair in the exam room while the doctor put the tongue depressor in my mouth, shone his little light down my throat, felt the glands in my neck.

Then he looked at me and said, "Just because you're hungry doesn't mean you have to eat your way through the entire grocery store." And that I'd "never get a boyfriend" if I didn't lose weight.

Maybe he said something about my throat or my fever. I don't remember. I do remember that my mom, her purse in her lap, said nothing. I do remember sitting on the edge of the examination table in my flimsy paper robe feeling like I'd been punched, spit on, my face shoved in the dirt. If all I'd felt was this hurt, and the anger that came with it, maybe I would have stuck up for myself. But the humiliation kept me as speechless as my mom.

Most of all I felt found out, like this stranger knew things about me no one else did: That I never stopped thinking about food or what I would eat next. That I always ate everything until it was gone because I couldn't stop. The times I'd stolen or hidden food to make sure I got it before anyone else did. How I read cookbooks and recipes like they were dirty magazines, transfixed by pictures of melting cheese or swirls of frosting, imagining how they would smell and taste and feel. The doctor seemed to know, too, that I worried there was nothing about me that might interest a boy.

We got my prescription for antibiotics and left. As we pulled out into traffic away from the hospital, my mom swore at another driver, something she hardly ever did. But she still didn't say anything about what the doctor had said; that he was right, or that he was wrong.

My grandma used to tell a story about me from when I was five or six. I'd stared at myself in the mirror for a long time, she said, and then spread my arms wide to declare (with my lisp) that my reflection was "gorgeouth!"

That's one piece of evidence that I once loved my

body, though it seems strange to think of it as "loving my body" since I didn't give it any real thought back then. I was my body and my body was me, not a separate thing I loved or hated or judged. My body was for doing things, like roller skating, playing foreign spy with the other kids in the neighborhood, dressing up like a princess or Laura Ingalls, running down the hallway of my best friend's apartment and leaping over stacks of pillows or sliding down her carpeted staircase in a slick nylon sleeping bag. I was in a children's ballet theater company and loved being onstage. In the fourth-grade school talent show, I did a rendition of "Movin' Right Along" from *The Muppet Movie* with a pretty girl named Rachael, complete with a big cardboard cutout of a taxi that we made ourselves.

By the fifth grade Rachael was lip-synching "Hit Me with Your Best Shot" in a black fringed leotard and fishnet stockings while I sang "Climb Every Mountain" with a group and worried that my terry-cloth dress showed too many bulges.

Certain words crept into the vocabularies of people around me—mostly adults who either didn't think I was listening or didn't care that these words were shaping my identity in a way that contributed to my feeling unsure and guilty about myself. They were words that judged my body: Husky. Chubby. Stocky.

No one came out and said it until sixth grade, when I was walking down the halls of my middle school and an eighth-grade boy looked right into my eyes and said, "You're fat."

• • •

I've always loved food. Always. It's a passion passed down to me by both my parents, but especially my father, who loved to eat and cook and serve food. Kid-friendly meals were not his specialty. Once I was sent away from the table for refusing a stuffed green pepper—not a favorite dish of nine-year-olds. He yelled at me, and I spent dinnertime on my bunk bed crying and feeling sorry for myself until he came into my room with his peace offering: a plate of saltines covered with butter and jelly. I could see the top of his balding head as he passed the plate to me on the upper bunk and watched me eat. The blend of creamy and salty and sweet took away the sting of being exiled from the table.

During times my dad was unemployed, we'd be home together in the afternoons and I'd sit at our yellow kitchen table while he brought me flour tortillas he'd buttered and then put under the broiler until they were puffed and brown. He'd make the best, greasiest pork chops for dinner, and serve up big patties of salty, sizzling corned beef at breakfast. We'd eat piles of pasta and yards of Polish sausage and ice-cream sundaes that filled soup bowls.

My dad was a man who had trouble with "I love you" or "I'm sorry." A plate of crackers with butter and jelly, or a perfect grilled cheese sandwich, was often the best he could do.

Eventually he wasn't there to cook for me anymore. Home alone in the afternoons while my mom worked, I'd duplicate my dad's recipes and invent my own. They usually involved some unholy combination of salty, fatty, and sweet: bologna dipped in mayonnaise, ramen noodles with cheese, bowls of cereal and milk with enough extra sugar to make a grainy sludge at the bottom of the bowl. Or I'd just eat candy that I bought at the corner store when I had money. When I didn't have money, I stole it. Which should have been a first clue that what I had wasn't so much a passion as a problem. Just like my dad's. I get that now. The same mix of genes and family history and depression that caused him to abuse alcohol caused us both to use food like a drug, use it for love, use it as a cure for boredom and loneliness.

Basically, I used it for everything, and by the time I was nineteen, I weighed two hundred pounds and hated myself for it.

The thing about hating my body is that my body contains me. It *is* me in the eyes of everyone on the outside. But when I was a teen and young adult, it felt like this *thing* my soul moved around in, and it was the *wrong* thing. In my mind I was a totally different person than my body said I was. The me of my interior had a certain kind of confidence, simmered with what I can only describe as *specialness* that I was desperate for people to notice. I wanted to make an impression on the world. I wanted people to see me. *Me.*

Ironically, fat people are often invisible. Especially the kind of fat person I was, in stretch pants and giant shirts and ugly shoes that kept my feet from hurting. I lived in San Francisco all through my twenties and schlubbed around town in my invisible-fat-girl clothes, letting people elbow me on the bus like I wasn't there or frown at me when I smiled at them. I never spoke up for myself if I was given bad service or got overlooked, or when someone was rude to me. That shame that had started back in fifth grade had developed into a full-on belief that by being fat, I'd forfeited my right to basic respect and decency—from myself or others. That I had to earn the space I took up by not rocking the boat. That the only way to buy my rights back was to lose weight. I took what that doctor said to heart and added to it: I would never get *anything,* didn't *deserve* anything, until I got thin.

I lived on the edge of a vast canyon. On the other side was the person I imagined as my true self. More than anything, I wanted to cross that canyon. I wanted to see the world from the other side, as the me I believed was there, somewhere, waiting for me to find her.

Shelley Winters and God came to my rescue.

One day in my late twenties I was home channel-surfing when I caught the 1972 movie *The Poseidon Adventure.* In it Shelley Winters plays a retired grandma with a good thirty or forty extra pounds. She's one of those invisible fat people in a plain dress; the other passengers hardly notice her at all. Until she saves their lives.

It turns out she used to be a champion swimmer. As the ship begins to sink, she's the only one who can hold her breath long enough to swim underwater and set up a rope that will lead them through an escape route. She swims, weightless, her dress floating away to reveal granny panties and thick legs. She's flabby armed and wrinkled. And strong. And beautiful.

I thought about that scene for days. How her body, exactly as it was, was in the shape it needed to be in for her to be a hero. If it had been me on that ship, would I have spoken up about my skills, *insisting,* as Shelley did, that the others let me save them? I don't think I would have, even to save myself. I'd be too afraid of not being heard or seen or believed, too scared they'd look at me and say, "You? *You?* But you're fat. What can *you* do?"

My fear and insecurity and detachment from my body were powerful enough to keep me from saving lives—even my own. I knew something had to change that wasn't about the number on the scale or the size of my clothes. Shelley reminded me that a body had a job to do, a job that wasn't about showing off cute outfits or looking hot by whatever standards of "hot" currently prevailed. A job that was more, even, than carrying around a soul. Not a thing separate from what's inside but a fully integrated part of what makes a whole person. That was a truth I'd known by instinct as a kid but lost somewhere between fourth and fifth, between the Muppets and the fishnets.

God's part came more slowly. I grew up in church, believed what I heard, and knew the story of Genesis backward and forward. But it wasn't until my Shelley Winters epiphany that I started to pay attention to that story in a new way. According to Genesis, as God created the world and humankind, he stopped every now and then to look at what he'd done. He "saw that it was good." Very good, even. The religion I've held dear all my life says that what God creates—including the body I'm in—is good. God doesn't qualify that statement. If I believe God made the giraffe with its long skinny legs and big eyes and "it was good," then I also have to believe that God made the round, short-legged guinea pig and that was good, too. The sleek, fast jaguar and the slow, crusty tortoise: both good. A deer? Good. An elephant? Also good.

So who decided that skinny and long limbed is more good than short and curvy? Or that the rock-hard abs of a body builder are more good than the lush stomach of a belly dancer? That a smaller nose is more good than a bigger one? Not God, apparently.

But you don't have to believe in God to get the point. An understanding of biology and evolutionary history led me to the same conclusion: that body types don't call for some kind of moral judgment of "right" or "wrong." They're determined by things set in motion eons ago by DNA, the landscape and climate of wherever my ancestors came from, whom my great-great-grandmother decided to marry. In other words, stuff I can't control. Just like I can't control the addiction-prone genes my dad passed down to me. Just like I can't get into a time machine and change the family dynamics that contributed to the way I abused food. And hating myself for things I can't control started to seem profoundly messed up. And definitely not helpful in dealing with my eating disorder.

And it is an eating disorder. For a long time I didn't think so. There were no TV movies or YA novels about what I had. Anorexia and bulimia, sure, but the obsessive thinking about food and eating it in huge volumes? That was just, well, being a glutton. I figured any self-respecting binge eater would at least have the decency to make herself throw up afterward. Maybe I had half an eating disorder. Maybe I was a bulimic who couldn't finish the job.

That's what I used to think, anyway, until the Internet came along to help connect the dots.

Somehow I found a group of women online who were, like me, trying to change the way they saw and used food and their bodies. A few of them had the same problems with compulsive eating that I did. A lot of them were older—middle-aged career women and overweight soccer moms. Some were younger and had serious problems like rheumatoid arthritis or debilitating injuries. None of us were looking for a diet or anyone to tell us what to do. What we wanted was to take back our bodies from the jerk doctors and middle-school bullies and destructive habits that had caused this crazy divorce between our bodies and our minds.

In one of my first posts to the e-mail list, I told my *Poseidon Adventure* story, and I couldn't believe the responses. It turned out I wasn't the only one to be inspired by Shelley and her heroic underwater swim. It was a Shelley Winters revolution. Before I knew it, not only was I inspired to work on taking control of my food issues, these women somehow convinced me to train for a 5K run while I was still nearly two hundred pounds. Within months I was among them in Golden Gate Park, most of us still fat, sporting our plus-size Spandex running pants and talking about run/walk intervals as if we had as much right as skinny people to be there running that race. At first I felt like I might get arrested for impersonating an athlete. But pretty soon I realized that there were all types of bodies in the crowd. Old people, flabby people, plain people, round people. And then the pack started moving, and there wasn't any more time to obsess about myself or how I looked in my shiny pants. I had a race to run.

The race gave me evidence about myself and the new identity taking shape.

It was evidence that though I may not have had any control over the things that set me up to have the body I had, I did have the power to take responsibility for it. Nothing was going to happen by magic or overnight, but I wasn't helpless.

It was evidence of the fundamental goodness of my body, that what I believed God said about creation—about me—was true. When I took care of myself, I saw that. As I took it a day at a time, eating moderately and getting exercise, my body did what I needed it to do, what it was made to do. Okay, so I wasn't a size two, or even a twelve, but I was already starting to sleep better and get sick less and have more energy.

It was evidence that I wasn't alone. I had some pretty significant issues, yeah, but there were other people out there with the same issues who were figuring out how to deal with them. That gave me hope for myself.

Most importantly, it was evidence that the me I wanted to be was not, in fact, on the other side of some vast canyon. She was right there with me, in me, *was* me. I knew that as, at the back of the pack with the snail's pace of a sixteen-minute mile, I crossed the finish line.

● ● ●

There is no finish line, though, when it comes to your body. You have it with you until the day you die. And even though I've lost about fifty pounds in seven years, it's not like I've permanently conquered anything. I still binge sometimes. There are still days I get sucked into my own drama, freak out, and wind up on the couch wallowing in shame, fear, and cookie-dough ice cream. But now I don't stay there, feeling helpless. I can't, because I no longer hate my body or see it as an enemy, and I want good things for it, for me.

I still think about that doctor. I wonder how many other girls he hurt by making them question their basic value and goodness, their very right to occupy space on the planet. I want to go back and tell him things, like how first of all you shouldn't go around assuming it's every girl's goal in life to "get a boyfriend." You shouldn't reduce her existence to that. And you shouldn't assume no one could possibly be attracted to a round body. I want to tell that doctor, tell *everyone,* about how shame is counterproductive. It might be a temporary motivator, but ultimately love is a better healer than shame or fear. I want to say how simple it really is to treat yourself with the same basic decency and kindness you'd show a friend. And how hard, too, but worth it.

Totally, completely worth it.

Pretty, Hungry

Ellen Hopkins

I Was a Preemie

Came into this world, scrapping and yowling,
all of three pounds, six ounces. Mom smoked
like a steel mill during the whole pregnancy.

Doc said that's why I was born early, why I
was so little. That didn't stop her smoking.
But it did explain tiny, squalling baby me.

The story, spread like bark beetles through our
family tree, and often shared, just within earshot of me, is that Daddy took one look, said,

> *She won't ever be a beauty, will she?*

Mom never even tried to breast-feed me, too
busy puffing away. Said she didn't want to
blow carcinogens in my scrunched-up face.

No, it was formula, day one. Anytime I fussed,
someone shoved a bottle in my mouth, and so I
learned the meaning of comfort food early on.

I Say "Someone"

Because my mom wasn't always around.
See, my dad was in the Navy (still is), and
when he was away, Mommy would play,
hanging out for hours in the local tavern.
Lucky for me, my grandmas were around.

Mom's mom, "Grandma" to me, has a nice
frame house on forty Kentucky acres. She
grows a garden while Grandpa Lou farms the
back twenty. Not much money in farming,
but plenty of love and home-grown food.

Daddy's mom, who I just call Gran, lives in
town, in a big brick house. She inherited a dime
or two when Grandpa Joe got killed in a cave-in.
Union mine workers' widows are well taken
care of. I spent lots of time in her kitchen, too.

From the day I came home from the hospital,
still small enough to nap in a boot box, Gran
and Grandma have played mother to me, and
a huge part of that game has been keeping me
fed. Which is how I grew into a behemoth.

Not That They Would Call Me That

Grandma has always called me "Buttercup."
A typical supper conversation: *Finish up*
those taters, Buttercup. And here's a little
more gravy to go with those biscuits and
sausages. How 'bout a big glass of milk?
Grandma, if I haven't mentioned it, weighs
maybe two seventy-five. She is a presence!

Gran calls me by my full baptized name.
Lorelei Jeanne! Come on down to dinner.
Roast turkey with all the fixin's. Wouldn't
want to see this bird get cold, now would
you? Here now, don't forget the skin. It's
the best darn part. Gran, who's the nervous
sort, weighs in right around two hundred.

So maybe you can understand how by
the time I started kindergarten, I looked
like someone should write "Goodyear"
across my behind. I took my fair share
of playground ribbing. By fifth grade
I was totally sick of it. But it wasn't my
peers who turned me around.

Daddy Came Home on Leave

Which meant I was at Mom's dilapidated
dwelling when he arrived. We were in the—
where else?—kitchen when he walked through
the door. It had been a while since he'd been
home, and at seeing his face, my heart felt
like it had doubled in size with happiness.
"Daddy!" I ran, reached him breathless.

He looked down at me, disgust in his eyes.
Is this my Lorelei? My, how you have grown.
The last word came out a stretched g-ee-rown.
Later, when I was supposed to be asleep, I
listened to the rant he directed at my mom.
You are supposed to be her mother, woman.
How could you let her get so damn heavy?

Mom mumbled something back about not
being my keeper. That set him off even more.
If you aren't her keeper, who the hell is? She
can barely cross the room without stopping
to catch her breath. It ain't healthy. And it
sure ain't pretty. You put that child on a diet
before she turns into a regular Bossy the cow.

His Words Bit

Like spider fangs. I loved Daddy
more than anything in the world.
And when he was away, I checked
off calendar days, one by one, until
he came home again. I lay in bed
that night, eyes swelling around
the tears, reciting my new mantra:

"I will be pretty. I will be pretty."

Daddy went back for another tour
of duty. Mom went back to her
tavern. And I went to Grandma's.
That night, when the taters came
round for the second time, I shook
my head. "No thank you." And
when Grandpa tempted me with a big

slice of apple pie, I let it pass on by.

Now, Grandma's McIntosh Divine
sure lives up to its name. Just a sniff
sets my mouth to watering. But I
kept hearing *Bossy the cow. She'll
never be a beauty, will she?* I shut
my mouth, repeated in my head,

"I will be pretty. I will be pretty."

No Seconds Wasn't So Bad

The no dessert thing was worse,
but I'd made up my mind. Then
I gave up milk in favor of water,
left a few bites on my plate. After
several months, my clothes fit
looser. I could walk to the bus
stop without getting winded.

People seemed nicer. Buddy
Lee almost quit making fun
of me. One day Grandma said,
Keep this up, Buttercup, you'll
turn into a regular beanpole.
No one loves a skinny girl.

Well, Grandpa surely did love
Grandma, but I guessed she
wasn't size twenty when he first
came to call. Still, I didn't think
mentioning that was the best
tactic. "The girls on TV are all
skinny. Everyone loves *them*!"

Movie stars. Supermodels.
Pop music divas. All of 'em
thinner than thin beanpoles.
Everyone *did* love them skinny.
And I was betting that my
daddy loved them best of all.

By Seventh Grade

I was what some people might
call pleasantly plump. Though
still nowhere near athletic, I
could manage to jog a whole
lap around the quarter-mile
track. PE wasn't a nightmare,
and most of the fat jokes were

aimed at someone besides me.
When Daddy came home for my
twelfth birthday, his eyes were
kinder. *Is this my Lorelei? I can
hardly recognize you. Who knew
you had cheekbones? Whatever
you've been doing, keep doing it.*

I ran to the mirror. Cheekbones!
Did that mean Daddy liked my
face? Every single scorned calorie
was so worth the hunger pangs.
A few more pounds, I'd have
rib bones. I could give up lunch
if it meant Daddy might stay.

See, He'd Decided

To divorce Mom. Budweiser
packs a heap of calories. She'd
drunk herself clear to "Bossy."
But more than that, Daddy had
lost patience with Mom's bleary-
eyed, molasses-tongued rants.
When he discovered her daily

tavern routine, he delivered a
stern ultimatum: clean up, dry
up, stay home, and play mother
or move out and shack up with
one of her booze buddies. When
he moved me to Gran's, I begged,
"Daddy, can't you please stay?"

> He shook his head, forced his
> voice gentle. *I have to go.*
> *I made a commitment to my*
> *country, and I am a man of*
> *my word. Remember, I'm not*
> *leaving you. It's your mother's*
> *bad habits that drove me away.*

I hated her after that. But
turned out Daddy was not
quite as honorable as he
claimed, and had a bad habit
of his own (not that I would
have believed it then)—
a woman in every port.

Life at Gran's

Wasn't so bad. I mean, I spent a lot of
                time there anyway. But I felt trapped.
Food was always an issue, always a
                major temptation. I even nibbled skin.
Then I'd start to feel guilty, start to
                worry about cheekbones. Rib bones.
If I got fat, he might go away forever.
                I weighed myself relentlessly. If I put
on a pound or two, I'd overcorrect,
                eating nothing but nonfat cottage cheese
and sugar-free applesauce until I lost
                four back. Gran would freak till I came
to my senses, started eating like a regular
                person again. I was a human seesaw.

I Started Eighth Grade

Weighing right around
one forty-five. Not bad
for five foot six, but not
great, either. Size 11,
comfy. Size 9 if I lay
on my bed to zip up, didn't

eat or drink a thing until
I unzipped again. When
Daddy returned that time,
he never asked about Mom,
who lived with a disabled
miner, helping the guy drink

his checks, trying to drown
the reality of his slow, sure
demise from black lung. But
Daddy didn't want to hear
about any of that, despite
Gran spreading gossip like

peanut butter. He ignored
her, focused instead on me.
*Look at Lorelei. She almost
has a real figure. Pretty soon
the boys'll come swarming.*
To my surprise, he was right.

Well, "Swarm"

Might be a slight exaggeration,
but a couple, maybe more,
started to take an interest
right about then, mostly
because, to my
absolute horror,
I sprouted boobs
that ballooned
into double Ds.

Buddy Lee's attention veered
in a whole different direction.
Instead of "Chubalub," he
took to calling me "Babe."
The name didn't
really bother me.
It felt positive, in
a dirty-old-man
kind   of   way.

If Buddy had had the sense
to tell me I was pretty, who
knows what I might have
let him do? He didn't
even try to kiss
me first. He just
went on and on
about my luscious,
humungous ta-tas.

Very Quickly

It became clear that luscious,
humungous ta-tas were not all
the movies made them out to
be. I decided to shed a few
pounds, hopefully drop a
cup size. The latest diet
craze was meat free.
Low fat. High
carb.

Of course, Grandma about
had a stroke, worried I'd drop
dead from protein deficiency.
And Gran: *No skin? Guess*
that means more for me. But
there ain't nothing wrong
with a little extra meat
on your bones,
hear?

I Heard, Didn't Listen

I bought *High Carb Your
Way to Waif,* followed
its strict instructions.
Veggies. Fruit. Whole
grains. Lots of water.

The diet had its desired
effect. I dropped a cup
size—two, in fact, plus
ten pounds of baby fat.
I started high school at

one thirty-five, ta-tas
stuffed into a healthy C
cup, the rest in size 7
jeans. I soon found plenty
of male attention, and I

quickly decided I liked
that. Almost as much
as I enjoyed the jealous
female sniping directed
my way. Jealous. Of me.

See, Friends Were in Short Supply

With all the shuffling back and forth
          between homes, I never developed

solid neighborhood buddies. And in
          school, being fat makes you a loner.

Lorraine was my one good friend,
          but she moved away in sixth grade.

And when your mom is a tavern
          tramp, her reputation rubs off on you.

Guys don't mind, of course, especially
          teenage guys. But the girls, oh they can

be cruel. They dished out elephant
          jokes for years. Then came "ho," before

I even knew what that meant.
          I sure couldn't spar with all of them.

So I took subtle revenge, tempting
          their boyfriends away from them.

Once the fat started melting away,
          that got easier and easier to manage.

A major milestone was my freshman
          year, when I scored Joshua Harper.

He Was a Junior

Going out with senior
class pres and drama
queen Shayna Gray.
I had hated her as long
as I could define hate.

Maybe that was because
she was nasty as snot.
Or maybe because she
was everything I wasn't.
Slender. Graceful. Popular.

One day right before
winter break, I was on
my way to algebra when
I bumped into Joshua,
exiting the chemistry lab.

My C-cup ta-tas came
to a solid stop against
Josh's six-pack. My face
flushed, heated. "Sorry."
But neither of us moved.

> He looked down into
> my eyes and smiled
> a smile that could melt
> Antarctica. *No problem.*
> *Hey. Do I know you?*

I laughed. "Kind of. Not
really. Your dad buys
hay from my grandpa."
Josh's sudden confusion
froze my smile in place.

Grandpa? He backed
away to study me. *No
way. You can't be that
little fa—uh—I mean, Lou
Layton's granddaughter?*

I laughed again. "That's
me. The little fat girl, in
the flesh. It's been a while
since you rode along out
to Grandpa's, I guess."

*Guess so. I can't believe
you're the same girl. You
look—* Just then Shayna
materialized. She called his
name, and he said, *Better go.*

I watched him join Ms.
Senior Class President,
who didn't notice the smile
he flashed over his shoulder.
It hit me like a torpedo.

Torpedoed!

At lunch I made a point
of walking by the senior
lawn, the place where
only seniors and their
invited guests could eat.

Shayna sat, straight as
a fence post, nibbling
a carrot stick. Posture,
I noted. Straighten spine,
tilt shoulders, lift chin.

Josh lounged in the grass,
head in Shayna's lap.
Envy stirred. Pretending
nonchalance, I studied
Shayna's narrow face.

Talk about cheekbones!
In fact, the obvious frame
beneath her flawless skin
totally defined her beauty.
I couldn't help but stare.

And she couldn't help
but notice. She looked at
me with arrogant eyes.
The smile that followed
was all the dare I needed.

Gran Barely Noticed

The new high-protein, zero-carb
          diet. I was eating meat and poultry,
including skin. Cheese, even.

          I hadn't touched much in the way
of potatoes or bread in quite a while,
          and my avoidance of fruit and veggies

completely slipped under her radar.
          I was manic about it, and every time
I happened to notice Shayna and Josh,

          I climbed even higher into the mania.
A single egg for breakfast. One
          slice of cheddar for lunch. I let myself

go at dinner—four ounces of
          roast or a chicken breast, a juice glass
of nonfat milk. Every time my

          tummy rumbled in traitorous protest,
I downed two big glasses of water.
          The H_2O helped the inevitable constipation,

but not quite enough. That's when
          I discovered the value of laxatives, and not
just to battle "stuck gut," as Gran called it.

As the Autumn Leaves Fell

So did the pounds.
At one twenty I had
an obvious frame,
killer cheekbones.
Size 5 butt, legs
like a racehorse.

        I no longer had to
        stuff my boobs
        into C cups. In fact,
        they just barely
        filled them, which
        was A–okay by me.

Guys checked me
out. A few asked
me out. I even said
yes to a couple who
Gran approved of
for some reason.

        If only she knew
        what they had on
        their split-pea brains.
        I started to feel sort
        of desirable. But I
        still didn't feel pretty.

One Day

The phone rang.
Lorelei? It's Josh.
I've got tickets to
Kenny Chesney.
Wanna go with me?

It took a sec to
catch my breath.
"Kenny Chesney?
Uh ... what about ... ?"
Turned out Josh
was many things,
but not a liar. Not
organized enough.

I could almost hear
his shrug. *She has*
to go to a wedding.
Anyway, it's not
like we're married
or something. So ...
what do you think?

When I hesitated,
he added, *By the*
way, have I told
you how great you
look? Whatever
you've been doing,
keep doing it.

Sold!

He hadn't exactly
called me pretty,
but *how great you
look* came close
enough. We went
to Kenny Chesney.

It was my first real
date and my first
real kiss and my
first real "almost."
In fact, it might
have been my first

real all the way,
except for one
major faux pas
on Josh's part.
We were right
there, on the edge,

when his cell rang.
Most guys would
know better than
to take a call from
their girlfriend while
making out with

another girl. Not
Josh. For someone
who wasn't *married
or something*, he sure
jumped to take her
call. That made me

so mad that
when he put a finger
to his lips, shushing
me, I decided not to
shush. "Tell Shayna
hi," I said loudly.

I didn't go out with
Josh again. But hey,
neither did Shayna.
And I kept on doing
what I'd been doing.
I guessed if Josh

thought I looked
great, with a little
perseverance, I'd
look even better—
good enough for
someone to call me

pretty.

The Next Time

Dad came home
was for Mom's
funeral. Booze
killed her before
black lung took
care of her miner.
Guilt hammered
all anger right

out of my heart.
See, Gran had sort
of convinced me
I was better off not
witnessing Mom's
alcoholic decline.
She was probably
right. But I never

had the chance to
tell Mom good-bye.
I know it's not
a new story. But
now it happens
to be mine, and
that will haunt my
dreams forever.

After the Burial

I was alone. Gran
had gone to the post-
burial potluck at
Grandma's house.
Despite my belly's
growling, I couldn't
bring myself to join
the boozing "dear
departed" toasting.
Dear departed Mom.

Daddy banged
through the screen
door, sat across
the kitchen table.
That's that, I guess.
He looked at me,
assessing, seemed
surprised at my tear-
striped face, puffed
up eyes. *You knew
it was coming.*

"Guess I did, but
if I'd known
how soon, I would
have tried to forgive
her while she was
still here to see me
do it. You know?"

He Didn't Answer Right Away

Just sat there staring
at me with his cool
steel gaze. I couldn't
meet his eyes so long.
It was the longest
time, in fact, we had
ever sat looking at
each other. At last
I had to look away.

        I heard the slide of
        his hand across the
        cracked Formica
        and, for the first time
        in longer than I could
        remember, felt the
        warmth of his skin as
        his fingers, tentative,
        tangled into mine.

        No use in grieving.
        She died a long time
        ago. He let his hand
        retreat, closed his
        eyes. *You look like*
        her. Just like she did
        the day I first saw her,
        bumping down that
        gravel road on Lou's
        big ol' John Deere.

Oh, she was a sight—
straight and slender
as a willow sapling,
with her corn-yellow
hair falling long
across her shoulders.
She looked at me with
such hope in those wide
green eyes, I wanted
to give her the world.
Keep looking like you
do—someone will want
to give the world to you.

It was the first and
only time Daddy ever
spoke of Mom like that.
My stomach growled,
and it came to me I
had not eaten in two
days. Nothing but a
few pieces of hard
candy. Didn't matter.
I might be hungry,
but for the first time
ever, I knew what
it was to feel pretty.

Daddy Left

The next day.
He's never
been one to
stay around
very long

Gran worries.
Some days
I don't eat
at all until
dinner, and
even then, I
mostly pick
at my plate.

I am thin
as a whisper
within my
ever-present
hunger, slim
as a willow
sapling.

Sometimes
my body
aches with
the most
basic need.

I Fight the Pain

Daddy never
spoke about
Mom again,
and I never
tried to get
him to. But
something
clicked that
day when he
went away,
an audible
snap inside
my brain.

For some-
one to love
me enough
to want to
give me the
world, I have
to be hungry.

Because
being
hungry
means
being
pretty.

How to Tame a Wild Booty

Coe Booth

My butt hit puberty before the rest of me. Before I was even ready.

I was eleven. From the front I looked my age—flat, skinny, awkward—but from the back I looked sixteen—curvy, sexy, with a booty that put the apple in "apple bottom." And we're talking BIG apple here!

I'm seventeen now.

My butt is twenty-six.

I'm never gonna catch up.

Not that I'm trying, really. I've given up on that. You would too if you could see the size of this thing. I mean, picture this: a girl who's just average in everything—

height, weight, looks—with smallish breasts and a well-defined waist, and a butt that just seems to come from nowhere. But there it is, all high and round and full. And huge. Did I mention *huge* already?

And that's my problem. I mean, like right now, I'm here trying to pack for freshman orientation. Three days living in a dorm, meeting people and previewing college life two months before I have to leave for the real thing. My mom bought me a five-piece luggage set for college, everything from the weekender bag to the twenty-nine-inch expandable upright, but I'm determined to travel light, to take only what I need. So I have the smallest suitcase open on my bed, which is covered with almost all the clothes I own, but I can't even figure out what to pack.

And why not?

Because of the booty. What else?

I mean, unlike other girls with normal-size butts, I can't just throw some clothes in a suitcase and get going. How can I when I'm gonna be meeting all these new people? It's like, if I choose the right clothes, for the first time in my life, maybe the first words out of everyone's mouth won't be "Man, look at that girl's butt!" I mean, how many times do I have to hear that?

That's the way it's been ever since I literally woke up one day with this, this *thing.* And it hasn't been easy. Even in my mostly black neighborhood, I'm not just another sistah-girl with too much going on back there. Even here I stand out. So what's it gonna be like at my new college, where the African-American population is a whopping six percent? Am I gonna be considered a *freak* or what?

I pick up a pretty sundress from off the bed, fold it, and

put it in the suitcase. It's a safe choice—cute, with enough flair not to hug any curves. Then I see a pair of shorts I've never worn before. For a second it feels good, freeing, to think of myself walking around campus in them, but then reality sets in. Who am I kidding? I can't wear shorts. I'm not allowed.

Haven't been allowed for years, ever since I was twelve.

It was one of the hottest days of the summer. I was hanging out with my friends in front of my building, listening to Destiny's Child and waiting for the ice cream truck to come around so I could get my daily toasted almond bar. I didn't own any shorts, so I was wearing a pair of my sister's cutoffs. They were a little tight on me—even though she's a year older, she's a size smaller—but the shorts fit, barely, so I wore them that day. I had to. It was *hot!*

Anyway, I was just minding my own business when this man from the next building came up to me and said something like "You growing up real nice, Stacie."

For a second I was stupid enough to think he was talking about my personality or something, and I almost smiled and said "Thank you." But then I noticed the gleam in his eyes and the way he was looking at my body, and all I could do was fold my arms in front of me and walk away from him. Fast.

I didn't see my father coming out of the building. Evidently, he had seen the whole thing, because the next thing I knew, he was screaming at the man, telling him that if he ever looked at me again, he would, let's say, chop off a certain part of the man's anatomy. My dad's reaction made me feel great. Protected. Well, until he turned to me and said, "Get inside. And don't ever let me see you wearing shorts again."

I was stunned. "What? What did *I* do?"

"Go!" he ordered, pointing to the door of our building, like I didn't remember where I lived.

But I wasn't done arguing. "You let Leanne wear these all the time!"

"You're not Leanne," he said. "Get upstairs, Stacie. Now."

It didn't matter to him that he was being completely unfair, blaming me for the way other people looked at me. My friends were gathered around me looking as shocked as I was but nobody said anything. Did I mention that my father is six feet four, two hundred forty pounds?

With nothing else to do, no other choice, I stomped away and went into the building, feeling the sun on my bare legs for the last time. *Ever.* I was so outraged. I mean, who did he think he was? The Taliban? Did he really think this was the only way he could protect me?

However unknowingly, he taught me the first trick for dealing with my "problem":

COVER IT UP

At first I protested, but pretty soon I started to believe my dad had the right idea. All those stares from the creepy men and all the ogling from the boys at school started to get to me, irritating me on a daily basis. A lot of girls in my class were doing all kinds of things to get that kind of attention. They were putting on too much makeup, wearing bras they didn't really need (and letting their bra straps *acci-*

dentally show, of course!), and they were shaking their non-existent hips whenever they walked through the halls.

The boys looked and smiled at them, but with me it was more extreme. They elbowed each other when I passed them, and they whispered too loud, things like "It looks like a basketball" and "Think we can bounce quarters off it?"

(The boys were really, *really* stupid in middle school.)

So I started doing what I could to conceal my *condition*. I wore baggy jeans and oversized sweatshirts that came all the way down to my knees. Or if I had on a T-shirt, it was always covered with a long men's shirt—ironically, one of my dad's.

When I was thirteen, my mom looked at me out of the corner of her eye one day and said, "I think you need a girdle."

I almost couldn't speak. It took a full minute for the breath to return to my lungs. *"What?"*

"A girdle," she said again, obviously not seeing the horrified look on my face. "Just to hold you in a little bit. Cut down on the, er, jiggle."

"A girdle?" I had to sit down for a second. "Like what *grandma* wears?"

"They have panty girdles now, Stacie, for younger women."

"I'm not a woman!"

"Well, no, not in *years,* you're not."

I knew what she was saying, that I had already become a woman . . . in my butt!

"I'm not gonna wear a girdle," I told her. "I don't even wanna hear that word again. It's just too . . . *weird.*" I stood up. "I'm going outside to play double dutch."

She didn't stop me, but I could see her shaking her head with concern as I left the apartment.

Of course outside on the sidewalk, as I jumped quickly between the two ropes, I could feel the "problem," the jiggle. I mean, even when I'd stop jumping, my butt would still kinda quiver up and down for a few seconds. Sorta like Jell-O. Why hadn't I noticed it before?

That weekend my mom and I went to Macy's. Not to the Juniors' department with all the exciting new, *young* fashions in it. No, we walked right past that section, to *Misses'*. And that's when I got it, my first—but not my last—girdle.

Freshman year of high school wasn't much better. I wanted to fit in so badly that nothing else mattered. Everybody at my school was wearing tight jeans and even tighter sweaters that year. Most of the school listened to the same radio station, all hip-hop all the time, and the morning DJ would announce the "slamming color" of the day, and everyone dressed accordingly, blindly. I mean, I would actually stand by the radio every morning at six thirty-five, half dressed, waiting to hear what color I was supposed to wear that day.

Anyway, one day, the slamming color was white. I wildly searched through my dresser for the one long, white sweater I owned, but I couldn't find it. Then I remembered my sister had borrowed it the week before and never returned it. Three minutes later I found it in the laundry basket with a ketchup stain on it, one that never came out.

Well, I couldn't go to school *un*slamming, so I just threw on a white T-shirt and finished getting dressed in a hurry. The only problem was, I forgot to wear one of my dad's long shirts over it. I left the house without even look-ing at myself in the mirror. I only remembered at the bus stop, when some man I didn't know eyed me up and down, paying extra-special attention to my butt, and said, "Hey, mama, how much do I need to ride?"

I put my hands on my hips and practically snarled, "Do I *look* like your mama to you?"

He held up his hands and said, "I was talking about the bus, that's all." Then he mumbled under his breath. "Can't blame a guy for looking."

For a second I considered running back home for something long enough to hide behind, just so I wouldn't have to put up with more perverted comments from men old enough to know better, but the bus was coming down the street and I didn't wanna get to homeroom late. So I went to school. And I tried to forget.

What a mistake! It was still early in my freshman year, and I had been in cover-up mode all semester, so this was the first time I had actually revealed my giant problem. And what I learned is that boys in high school were a lot *cruder* than they had been the year before. They looked at me with eyes that practically displayed their thoughts in high definition. I knew what they were thinking about. And it was kinda scary. I mean, I wasn't my body. My butt didn't define me.

But the truth was, it kinda did. At least as far as the guys at school were concerned. By sixth period I'd been slapped on the butt three times, been pinched once, and gotten many offers to share my *goods* with certain members of the basketball and football team. It was humiliating. Not one of those guys knew me, not even my name, but all of a sudden I was on their radar. And I didn't like it one bit. I mean, I wanted the guys to like me, sure, but for *me*.

With nothing to cover myself up with, I felt exposed and open and *vulnerable* all day. But what could I do? What was I *supposed* to do? Spend my whole life hiding my body? My*self*? No. If I didn't like my body, then I had to do something about it.

It was that day I figured out a better way to overcome my particular problem:

GET RID OF IT

That's right. The booty, like all parts of my body, was made up of (among other things) muscle and fat. In my case, *a lot* of fat. And fat was something I could burn off, or at least shrink down a bit. It was all simple, after all. A little less food. A lot more exercise. All it took was will power and discipline. And if I stuck with it, my problem would be gone. Right?

As soon as I made up my mind, I remember getting a little bang of fear. If my plan worked and I lost the excess weight in my behind, what would I look like? Would I just blend in with all the other girls? Would I lose some of what made me special? I mean, who would I be without my big butt?

It was all too much to think about. But I took on the challenge, and for the next several months I worked hard to create a new me. I cut out the snacks and all the really fattening foods I'd never thought twice about eating, like cheese and bacon, things everyone told me went straight to the butt. I stayed after school for open gym three days a week to use the treadmill and the Butt Blaster machine. I thought I was doing everything right. I was dedicated without being obsessed. I weighed myself only once a week so I wouldn't put too much emphasis on the numbers but instead on how I felt and how my clothes fit.

I even met Marcus in the gym. Well, I'd known him since school started, but we'd never talked before. He was in my world literature class, but he sat on the other side of the room and always looked bored, no matter what we were talking about.

He was cute, though. I noticed that on the first day of class. He was tall and thin, with deep brown skin and a smile that made everyone wanna be in on the joke. The thing I liked about him was he wasn't flashy like some of the other guys at my school. He was cool and confident.

I never thought a guy like him would even look at me, but he did. Open gym wasn't exactly the most popular after-school activity, so sometimes there would only be about five or six of us there. My friend Kim said she would work out with me, but after two weeks she started coming up with excuses. But I wasn't gonna let her lack of commitment discourage me. So I went by myself one day, and that's when Marcus decided to make his move.

It was kinda embarrassing, though. There I was on all fours, pushing my leg back and up against the weight of the Butt Blaster, sweating and counting out loud, when he walked across the room toward me and leaned against the mirror. "How many are you doing?" he asked.

I was so out of it, I just said, "I'll be done with the machine in a few minutes."

"No," he said. "I was just going to tell you that you might want to use less weight and increase your reps."

"*You* were using heavy weights over there on that chest machine," I said, immediately realizing that he now knew I'd been watching him.

"Yeah, but I'm trying to bulk up, you know, get some muscle. But you don't want to increase the size of—"

The silence that followed was so long and so uncomfortable, I did the only thing I could to break it. I laughed. Then he smiled that beautiful smile and laughed with me.

"I didn't mean anything by that," he said, sitting down on the mat.

"I know," I said, crawling out of the machine and joining him, leaning against the mirror.

"And a skinny guy like me shouldn't even be giving out exercise tips."

"You're not skinny," I said, using that opportunity to get a good look at him from top to bottom. "You're good."

"So are you," he told me, and it sounded like he meant it.

I shook my head. "No, I'm not. I wanna lose a little weight and get my body in the right . . . proportion."

"It looks right to me," he said. And there was that smile again. And that was it. I was hooked.

Working out with Marcus after school made the whole "exercise thing" a lot more fun. We didn't use the same machines since our goals were so different, but when I was on the treadmill, I knew he was watching me, and that made me run faster, work harder.

Marcus never understood why I was focusing so much

on one part of my body. He tried to get me to stop covering myself up all the time, to stop wrapping a jacket around my waist when we went out on dates, especially when it was so warm outside there was no need for one. But old habits die hard. After so many years, I felt naked when I wasn't hiding my body under unnecessary clothes.

After a couple of months on Operation BBG (Booty Be Gone), I had lost a noticeable amount of weight, but not one single ounce of it came off my butt. In fact, with my waist suddenly so small, my behind looked three, possibly *four,* times bigger. I mean, on more than one occasion some jerk in the cafeteria asked if he could put his drink on my *shelf.* Yeah, the guys were *so* funny.

But I can't tell you how frustrating it was to work so hard and get the exact opposite result. Even I had to admit that I looked positively deformed. And with my skinnier body, I barely had the strength to lug the *thing* around. It was exhausting. I mean, it felt like I was carrying around luggage all the time.

Marcus and I dated for the rest of freshman year. He didn't gain any muscle and eventually gave up on lifting weights. He said he had to learn to accept himself the way he was. Tall and skinny. It wasn't so bad.

I wanted to accept myself, too. I wished I could just walk around freely without all the layers, but I couldn't. I wasn't ready. Maybe I was scared.

The thing is, even with Marcus I couldn't let my guard down. He never pressured me for sex, but even the thought of him touching me made me so . . . tense. I was in ninth grade. I should have been ready for some kind of intimacy, right? But every time we were alone together, I kept thinking about those grown men and how they'd looked at me all those years ago. And those boys in school who only noticed one thing about me.

I trusted Marcus. I didn't wanna lump him in with the others, but a part of me was still hurt and angry. What had I done to deserve all that disgusting attention? I mean, that kind of thing changes a person.

Marcus and I grew apart the summer before sophomore year. When we broke up, I was deeply sad and thoroughly relieved at the same time. I wasn't ready to be in a relationship. Not back then.

Actually, three years later, I'm still not ready. Sure, I've dated, but nothing serious. I've felt a little more comfortable around the guys I dated since Marcus, though, because I no longer had the problem to deal with. Not really. Because after I lost all the weight, and after I lost Marcus, I discovered the best way to mend a broken heart and rid myself of my problem area once and for all.

CAMOUFLAGE IT

Covering it up gets a little annoying after a while, and losing it is way too much work. I mean, how long can a person survive without ice cream? It's just not normal. After I broke up with Marcus, all I wanted was sweet, fattening, *comforting* foods. The more the better. It was great! Breaking up with your first boyfriend provides a built-in excuse to let yourself go. And yes, I know, in theory that period of time is supposed to end, but after denying myself for so long, I had a lot of making up to do.

Then, as I gained the weight back, and kept gaining

and gaining, I stumbled upon a bright side to everything. *A miracle.* The bigger I got, the less my butt stood out. Yes, it was big—enormous, even—but *I* was big, too! I wasn't a freak. Oh, no! I was just another chubby girl with a big behind. And you know what? I could live with that.

By the end of sophomore year all those oversized clothes I used to cover myself up with fit me perfectly. And there was no reason to run out and buy even bigger clothes to hide in. I was free for the first time in years.

This is not to say that the guys didn't still look at me. I was an okay-looking girl, even with fifteen or twenty extra pounds, but I no longer felt as exposed as I used to. The extra weight felt like a little bit of protection from their stares. I was buried inside a soft shell, and I could relax in there because nobody could see me.

Hiding behind the extra weight got me through high school, but slowly over the past couple of months I've returned to my normal weight. And yes, the weight loss brought my butt back to the attention of everybody, *everybody,* but I'm seventeen and I can handle it a little better.

But I still can't decide what to take with me to freshman orientation. I hate that this part of my body still makes me have to stop and think. And *feel.* There's just so much history here, so much weighing me down. And I wanna be the one in charge of my own image at college.

I throw a pair of jeans into my suitcase and immediately, almost on impulse, follow it with a long, dark T-shirt. Then, a second later, I throw in a shorter T-shirt, just in case I don't feel like covering up. Then I pick up that pair of shorts again and stare at them, turning them over, back to front, front to back, a couple of times.

My sister comes into my room and sits on the edge of my bed—the only space available—and says, "It's just three days. You can't take everything you own, you know."

"I know," I say, still looking at the shorts. They're really cute. Deep maroon with a tiny flowery design on the back pocket. And the price tag is still on them, dangling proof that I've never had the nerve to put them on before. Well, maybe I *can* wear them . . . if I go back to tying a jacket around my waist. That might work.

"You're gonna need one of the bigger suitcases," Leanne says, laughing. "Mom bought you enough of them, don't you think?"

"No," I say, throwing the shorts in and zipping the suitcase fast before I can add that jacket. I grab the suitcase off the bed and hurry to my bedroom door. "I don't wanna take too much stuff with me. I have enough baggage as it is."

And maybe that's it. After so many years. I'm practically in college now. Maybe the solution to this problem is easier than I thought. Maybe it's finally time to just:

FLAUNT IT!

Confessions of a Former It Girl

as told to *Wendy Shanker*
at the Chateau Marmont in Hollywood

Sorry I'm late. I wasn't gonna come, and then I thought I had to, and then I thought I shouldn't, and then I started watching season nine—I mean, CYCLE nine of *America's Next Top Model,* and then I was like: What the hell, and here I am.

I definitely should NOT be here. This is, like, dangerous. I swear, there's a set of tiny identical twins that would KILL ME for even e-mailing you back. But my sponsor—sorry, my sober companion—said that it would be good for me, and part of my healing, to explain why I did what I did, so I'm doing it.

I'm ninety-one days into my celebrity sobriety. But every time I walk by a newsstand, I want to pick up *Us Weekly* and rip on people inside. I had to delete Perez Hilton from my bookmarks. Sometimes I get in my car and drive past a Pinkberry just to see the logo. And no more Starbucks for me. My sponsor—sorry, my sober companion—told me that I'm not allowed to have Frappuccinos. She says they're "trigger drinks."

I just want to say for the record that I'm not that different from you, or that waiter over there, or that woman walking by wearing only the thong and the baby T— okay, maybe I'm different from her. Now. So weird out here, isn't it? L.A. is nuts. All these pretty people sitting together, just . . . looking pretty. What do those pretty couples TALK about? How pretty the other one is? And everyone looks funny, not like ha-ha but like a little off or something. It's all the plastic surgery. The moms look younger than the daughters. I keep thinking, if a mom and a dad have all that surgery so they can look different from their original selves, what happens when they have a kid who looks like the old, ugly them? Will the kid even recognize them? Or will they start doing plastic surgery on the kid in the delivery room? I think about this stuff now.

I was a regular kid. Average. Grew up in the 'burbs in Cleveland. Nice parents, little brother, nice house, all that stuff. I always thought I was kind of pretty and smart, and then when I turned twelve or thirteen I was suddenly like BARF. I got massively uncute. It was so awful. It didn't matter how many times I straightened my hair, or went on a diet, or started Proactiv. I was a mess, and not special, and

I really wanted to be special, you know? I wanted to be noticed. Nobody cares about how funny you are, or if you can play drums or do math or write for yearbook or any of that stuff. It's all about how you look. I was always afraid I'd be watching an *Oprah* about fat people and see myself on it as one of those people they only show from the waist down walking around and eating hot dogs on the street. Aren't you terrified of that? What if you see one of those fat asses on TV and recognize yourself?

Now I look back at videos and pictures of myself when I was thirteen and think I looked just fine. But at the time? Whoa. Everyone was so much hotter than me! Not just the girls at school, although Alyssa Van Deemer was always blond and perfect and probably still is. I'm talking about every girl on a magazine cover, every movie star, all the kids on Nick or in *Teen Vogue* or the notfat ones from *American Idol*. Guys thought those girls were hot, and girls wanted to be their friends, and I think even parents wondered why we couldn't be that way too: pretty and talented and rich and kind of crazy and all that stuff. It makes no sense. You have to look slutty but not be slutty. Act not smart but be smart. Care but not care. So stupid. But what—I'm gonna be the one that changes the system? I'm gonna be the one that puts up a fight? It's how things ARE.

The weird thing is that famous people—who, by the way, are not regular human beings living regular lives—are desperate to prove how NORMAL they are. They go to the beach, and they go on reality shows, and they pump their own gas. Still not normal. Not normal to have photographers following you in the supermarket, or paying your best friend to be your assistant, or getting all your clothes for free, or hiring your mom be your manager. Momager. Whatever. Not the way it should be. But it sure looked yummy at the time.

Celebrities seemed to know a secret that I wasn't in on. Clearly it wasn't about talent. There are so many people who are famous for being famous. It was like there was someone you could know or something you could buy that would make you BETTER. That would FIX you. And then you would be perfect and happy and everyone would LOVE you. Who doesn't want that?

I deferred college and came out here. I didn't want to end up at my high school reunion and be LAME. Before I knew it, I became addicted to celebrity. Not just being a celebrity, but knowing about celebrities. Their lives became more important than my own. I'd click right to the entertainment section and never read the front page. Celebrities were my life. I wanted to be like them and act like them and look like them. Now obviously I know that there's a lot of sick stuff going on in that world. I mean, how badly do you need attention if you HACK OFF YOUR HAIR in public? And what do you do to top that—kill a guy?

With me, it started small. One day I wore sunglasses indoors. Now I know that was "gateway" behavior. At the time it just seemed like a style statement. But everyone wears sunglasses indoors, so I tried something else to get attention. I started speaking in a lower, more gravelly voice.

Still, nothing. Not famous yet. So I started carrying a Starbucks with me wherever I went. I would complain about all the calories in a Frappuccino but make sure I never drank any. That cup was always full. At night I switched to Red Bull.

But nobody noticed.

So I lied about my age.

I plucked off all my eyebrows.

I hijacked my own Sidekick.

I bought a Chihuahua and named it Pinky.

I designed my own fashion line.

I got dehydrated and went to the E.R.

I got a tattoo.

I rented a house in the Hamptons.

I flashed myself with a camera whenever I got bored.

I ate only yellow food. Then red food. Then purple food. (There's not a lot of purple food out there, by the way. It's like, eggplant and grapes and call it a day.)

Nada.

I kissed my brother.

People noticed that.

So I adopted a kid from Bali.

I had a quickie marriage in Vegas that got annulled the next day.

I bought an Escalade and drove it into a tree.

I dated John Mayer.

I got drunk and put a video of myself on YouTube.

I pounded Milky Ways so I could go on *Celebrity Fit Club*.

I got gastric bypass surgery but told everyone I lost weight from the flu.

I stole a bunch of crap from Saks.

I made a sex tape.

I went to jail for forty-seven hours.

I called 911 just so I could hear my voice on the news.

I stopped wearing underwear. And started showing people.

The buzz was on. And everyone around me encouraged it!

So I had my eyes lifted, my ears pinned, my hair extended, my nose shaved, my cheeks raised, my boobs implanted, my lips plumped, my tummy tucked, my vagina waxed, my legs lengthened, my knees lipoed, my toes removed, my arches modified, my nails tipped, my arms resected, my butt heightened, my thighs tightened, my forehead flattened, my glutes enhanced, my eyes Lasiked, my smile Botoxed, and my teeth Zoomed.

I was in the zone.

So I hired a trainer, went to an ashram, learned tai chi, practiced yoga, studied karate, and tried hand-to-hand combat with an Israeli paratrooper. I went vegan, then drank only maple syrup, then ate only bacon and Babybel cheese. I dropped Kabbalah and converted to Scientology. I joined a boxing-only gym, climbed Mount Everest, and entered a Tibetan monastery.

At that point everyone knew about me.

So I moved to Paris, runway modeled, won the X Games, divorced my parents, sued my therapist, wrote a painful tell-all autobiography, channeled Marilyn Monroe, became Quentin Tarantino's muse, recorded a country pop album, did a duet with Diddy, tried smack, kicked smack, and lived in a tree for seven and a half months without letting my feet touch the ground to bring awareness to the destruction of the environment. Good times.

Most people say I hit rock bottom the night that I got bleeped at the Oscars and then slugged Ryan Seacrest at the Governor's Ball. But I consider that more of a cry for help. Truth is there is no rock bottom with this celebrity stuff. There's just stepping off the edge and free-falling forever.

Finally there was an intervention. My brother and his wife came in from Cleveland. My old friends showed up from high school. They sent me to rehab. Not like drug rehab, but more like fame rehab. There were pop starlets, and members of boy bands, and celebutantes, and former child stars, and leading men. Everyone had stories about drugs and rejection and compromise and repression and never, ever eating any ice cream. After twenty-eight days in Utah, I had to come home and unmake the mess I had made of my almost-famous life.

So I bought all of my own stuff back on eBay.

I deleted all the people I knew only by their first names from my cell phone.

I pulled the red carpet off of my front walk.

I had the stripper pole removed from my house.

I took down my cover photo from *Maxim* that I had blown up over my fireplace (number 73 on the *Maxim* Hot 100—not bad!)

I returned the wax model of myself to Madame Tussaud's.

I fired my mom.

I ate carbs.

Now I really am normal. Regular. I go to work, hang out with some friends, window-shop. I applied to college again. Gonna try the Natalie Portman route this time.

This is a cautionary tale. It could happen to anyone. It ended up happening to me. Now I'm normal. And I WANT to be normal.

Well, normal—but not average.

Do you think I can do it?

Do you think you can help?

Supplements

Sample Sale: Books That Fit

Life in the Fat Lane, Cherie Bennett: "The old me shopped with my friends. The new me shopped alone."

Blubber, Judy Blume: "Whales are loveable animals . . . skeletons are just dead, bony things."

Staying Fat for Sarah Byrnes, Chris Crutcher: "As a fat kid growing up I just assumed there would never be a girl for me."

Just Listen, Sarah Dessen: ". . . she was breathtaking. So much so that it was hard to believe she could ever have looked at herself and seen anything else."

The Looks Book, Esther Drill, Heather McDonald, Rebecca Odes: "Your body is yours alone."

Fat Kid Rules the World, K. L. Going: "I am the Rocky Balboa of obese drummers."

Little Miss Tiny, Roger Hargreaves: "She was so very tiny she didn't live in a house."

One Fat Summer, Robert Lipsyte: "I always hated summertime. When people take off their clothes."

Yell-Oh Girls! Emerging Voices Explore Culture, Identity, and Growing Up Asian American, edited by Vickie Nam: "I was a gyo-po in Korea, a foreigner in the States. So where was my country?"

Holes, Louis Sachar: "Some teachers even seemed to find it amusing that a little kid like Derrick could pick on someone as big as Stanley."

Lucy the Giant, Sherri L. Smith: "It doesn't help to be my size when someone wants to ignore you."

Forever in Blue: The Fourth Summer of the Sisterhood, Ann Brashares: "You must never say the word 'phat' while wearing the Pants. You must also never think to yourself, 'I am fat' while wearing the Pants."

Girls Under Pressure, Jacqueline Wilson: "'Ellie can't have that slimming disease thingy,' says Egg. 'She isn't thin, she's fat.'"

Body Outlaws: Rewriting the Rules of Beauty and Body Image, edited by Ophira Edut: "It seems like everybody has an opinion when it comes to my hair."

Big Girls Don't Cry— They Dance!: A Playlist

"Big Girl (You Are Beautiful)"—Mika, *Life in Cartoon Motion*

"Gut Feeling"—Devo, *The Life Aquatic with Steve Zissou: Soundtrack from the Motion Picture*

"Lose Control"—Missy Elliott Feat. Ciara & Fat Man Scoop, *The Cookbook*

"Dress Up in You"—Belle and Sebastian, *The Life Pursuit*

"That Old Pair of Jeans"—Fatboy Slim, *The Greatest Hits: Why Try Harder*

"Lost in the Supermarket"—The Clash, *London Calling*

"I Eat Cannibals"—Total Coelo, *I Eat Cannibals and Other Tasty Trax*

"Vogue"—Madonna, *The Immaculate Collection*

"Supermodel"—Jill Sobule, *Jill Sobule*

"Big, Blond and Beautiful"—Queen Latifah, *Hairspray: Soundtrack from the Motion Picture*

"Let the Cool Goddess Rust Away"—Clap Your Hands Say Yeah, *Clap Your Hands Say Yeah*

"My Body Is a Cage"—Arcade Fire, *Neon Bible*

"Shake"—Ike & Tina Turner, *The Very Best of Ike & Tina Turner*

"Celebrity Skin"—Hole, *Celebrity Skin*

"Bodyrock"—Moby, *Play*

"Banquet"—Bloc Party, *Silent Alarm*

"You're Pretty Good Looking (For a Girl)"—The White Stripes, *De Stijl*

"Nightswimming"—R.E.M., *Automatic for the People*

"Hang Me Up to Dry"—Cold War Kids, *Robbers & Cowards*

"Some Girls Are Bigger Than Others"—The Smiths, *The Queen Is Dead*

Ugly Betty Not On?
Try These

●

Bridget Jones's Diary: Renée Zellweger gained twenty pounds to play Bridget, and Colin Firth and Hugh Grant fought over her.

Circle of Friends: Minnie Driver also gained weight for this role, and she, too, gets the guy in the end.

The Color Purple: One word: Oprah! Okay, more than one word. Alice Walker wrote the book, one of my favorites, and the movie lives up to it. Whoopi Goldberg shines as Celie, a woman who gradually learns to love herself, thanks, in part, to Oprah's character.

Dreamgirls: American Idol* finalist Jennifer Hudson brought it, and won an Oscar.

Drop Dead Gorgeous: A spot-on black comedy set behind the scenes at a beauty pageant. Great cast.

Edward Scissorhands: When you're feeling bad about your body, think of poor Edward and his scissor hands.

Hairspray: Good morning, Baltimore! The original movie launched Ricki Lake's career; the recent musical starred newcomer Nikki Blonsky and Queen Latifah.

Mask: A mother (Cher) learns important lessons from her son, who has a facial deformity.

Muriel's Wedding: Toni Collette, the mom from *Little Miss Sunshine,* and ABBA's music star in this Australian film about finding yourself (and your soundtrack).

Phat Girlz: Check out Mo'Nique in this comedy and on her Oxygen show, *Mo'Nique's F.A.T. Chance,* her answer to Tyra's *Top Model.*

Real Women Have Curves: America Ferrera made her film debut in this award winner. The sewing-shop scene is fabulous.

Super Size Me: This guy ate McDonald's every day, for every meal, for a month. The results? Not so good.

Titanic: Thank you, Kate Winslet. Later, when a magazine digitally altered her cover photo to make her look thinner, she came out and said they had done it without her consent.

The Truth About Cats & Dogs: The truth about this movie: Janeane Garofalo's character is clearly so much more appealing than Uma Thurman's.

Size These Sites Up

Adios, Barbie: adiosbarbie.com

Be a bathing beauty: maliamills.com

Big Fat Blog: bigfatblog.com

Dove Campaign for Real Beauty: campaignforreal-
beauty.com

Eating disorder info: nationaleatingdisorders.org

Find your perfect jeans: zafu.com

Full-figured fashion: beautypluspower.com, torrid.com

Girls' bill of rights: girlsinc.org/about/girls-bill-of-rights

Gurl power: gurl.com

Health is wealth: iemily.com

Performance art: lesliehall.com

Punk goddess: Beth Ditto: myspace.com/gossipband

Rock (not fat) camp: williemaerockcamp.org

Stick out: stickersisters.com

Supermodel: emmestyle.com

Things I Could Have Done Instead of Worrying About My Weight . . .

Lauren R. Weinstein

About the Contributors

Daniel Pinkwater is the author of about a hundred books, mostly for children and young people. He has been a popular commentator on National Public Radio since 1987.

Size: XXXL

Megan McCafferty is the *New York Times* best-selling author of the comic coming-of-age novels *Sloppy Firsts, Second Helpings, Charmed Thirds,* and *Fourth Comings.* And don't miss *Perfect Fifths,* the fifth and final book in the Jessica Darling series. Her work has earned honors from the American Library Association and the New York Public Library and has been translated into ten languages, including Hungarian, Turkish, and Japanese. Before she was a novelist, Megan wrote and edited numerous articles about body image for teen and women's magazines. She lives with her husband and son in New Jersey. Find out how Megan felt about her adolescent appearance by reading her real teenage-era journals on her (retro)blog via www.meganmccafferty.com.

Size: S

Eireann Corrigan hopes that her obsession with the TV show *The Biggest Loser* doesn't interfere with her recovery. To be fair, she also loves *Top Chef.* Eireann attended Sarah Lawrence College and then earned her master's degree at NYU. She has published three books: *You Remind Me of You* (Scholastic, 2002), *Splintering* (Scholastic, 2004), and *Ordinary Ghosts* (Scholastic, 2007) She lives in New Jersey with her husband, her cats, and a cupboard full of cupcakes.

Size: M

Matt de la Peña's debut novel, *Ball Don't Lie,* was published by Delacorte in 2005. The novel is soon to be released as a major motion picture starring Ludacris, Nick Cannon, Emelie de Ravin, Grayson Boucher, and Rosanna Arquette (Night and Day Pictures). In the fall of 2008 de la Peña's second novel, *Mexican WhiteBoy,* was released by Delacorte. He has published fiction in various literary journals, including *Pacific Review, The Vincent Brothers Review, Chiricú, Two Girls Review, George Mason Review,* and *Allegheny Literary Review.* He received his MFA in creative writing from San Diego State University and his BA from the University of the Pacific, where he attended school on a full basketball scholarship. De la Peña currently lives in Brooklyn, New York, and teaches creative writing workshops all over New York City.

Size: XL

Wendy McClure grew up in Oak Park, Illinois, where an awful lot of television sitcoms are set. She holds an MFA in poetry from the University of Iowa. She is the author of the memoir *I'm Not the New Me,* based in part on her weblog at www.poundy.com. Additionally, she is a columnist for *Bust* magazine, and her writing has appeared in the *Chicago Sun-Times, The New York Times Magazine*, and several anthologies. She lives in Chicago.

Size: XXL

Sarra Manning started her career at the legendary United Kingdom teen magazine *Just Seventeen* as entertainment editor. Sarra then joined the launch team of *Ellegirl UK* and took over the editorship. Sarra has also been editor of the BBC fashion title *What to Wear*.

Sarra left full-time magazine publishing after the success of her teen novels *Guitar Girl, Pretty Things,* and *Let's Get Lost.* Her books have been published in the United States, France, Germany, Sweden, Italy, Denmark, Brazil, and Holland. Sarra is now a contributing editor for British *Elle* and also writes for *Grazia, Red, The Guardian,* and *The Sunday Telegraph's Stella* magazine.

Sarra's latest teen series, *Fashionistas,* has just been published in the United Kingdom, and she's currently writing *Unsticky*, her first "grownup" novel. Find out more at http://sarramanning.blogspot.com.

Size: M

Margo Rabb's novel *Cures for Heartbreak* was published by Delacorte and named one of the Best YA Books of 2007 by *Kirkus Reviews* and ALA *Booklist.* Her stories have been published in *The Atlantic Monthly, Zoetrope: All-Story, Seventeen, Mademoiselle, Best New American Voices, New Stories from the South, New England Review, Glimmer Train, One Story,* and elsewhere, and have been broadcast on National Public Radio. She received the grand prize in the *Zoetrope* short story contest, first prize in the *Atlantic Monthly* fiction contest, first prize in the *American Fiction* contest, and a PEN Syndicated Fiction Project Award. Visit her online at www.margorabb.com.

Size: XS

Jaclyn Moriarty grew up in Sydney, Australia, flew away to live in the United States, England, and Canada, and then went home to Sydney again. She once worked as a media and entertainment lawyer but now spends her days taking her baby, Charlie, to the park, and writing whenever Charlie sleeps. Jaclyn is the author of the international bestseller *Feeling Sorry for Celia* and its companion books, *The Year of Secret Assignments* and *The Murder of Bindy MacKenzie*. Her most recent novel is *The Spell Book of Listen Taylor.* You can see photographs of Charlie at www.jaclynmoriarty.com.

Size: "That depends who I'm standing next to."

Carolyn Mackler is the author of the award-winning teen novels *The Earth, My Butt, and Other Big Round Things* (a Michael L. Printz Honor Book), *Guyaholic, Vegan Virgin Valentine,* and *Love and Other Four-Letter Words.* Her novels have been published in numerous countries, including the United Kingdom, Australia, Germany, France, Italy, Korea, the Netherlands, Denmark, Israel, and Indonesia. Carolyn has contributed to *Seventeen, CosmoGIRL!, Glamour, Girls' Life,* and *American Girl.* She lives with her husband and young son in New York City. Visit her online at www.carolynmackler.com.

Size: M

Barry Lyga grew up thinking he was a fat kid, but when he looks back at pictures from high school, all he sees is a skinny kid. Weird, huh? He is the author of *The Astonishing Adventures of Fanboy & Goth Girl* and *Boy Toy.* He used to work in the comic-book industry, but now he writes full-time. Every now and then, though, someone manages to rope him into writing a comic again . . . like this time. Visit him online at www.barrylyga.com.

Size: M

Born with the unique ability to create amazing works of art, **Jeff Dillon** honed his abilities at the Maryland Institute College of Art. World-weary and war-torn, he continues looking for different ways to utilize his unique abilities. Jeff's works can be found online, in print, and on friends' and families' walls. He currently lives in Baltimore with his wife, Sonomi.

Size: M

Sara Zarr is the author of two young adult novels: the National Book Award finalist *Story of a Girl* and *Sweethearts*. She lives in Salt Lake City, Utah, the birthplace of fry sauce, which Sara regularly enjoys without guilt.

Size: M

Ellen Hopkins is the *New York Times* best-selling author of *Crank, Burned, Impulse,* and *Glass.* She lives in Carson City, Nevada, with her husband, son, three German shepherds, and three ponds (not pounds) of fish. Learn more than you ever wanted to know about her at www.ellenhopkins.com.

Size: S

Coe Booth is the author of *Tyrell,* winner of the *Los Angeles Times* Book Prize for Young Adult Fiction, and *Kendra,* both published by Push. She lives in the Bronx, where she writes full-time. For more information on Coe, check out her website: www.coebooth.com.

Size: XL

Wendy Shanker's humorous, hopeful memoir about women and body image, *The Fat Girl's Guide to Life* (Bloomsbury USA), changed the way many women related to their weight. You may have seen Wendy discussing her book on *The View, Good Morning America,* or *CBS Sunday Morning* or on her national tour sponsored by Macy's. *The Fat Girl's Guide* has been published in nine languages, including Italian, German, and Chinese (but not French—because French women don't get fat).

Wendy's byline has appeared in *Glamour, Self, Shape, Us Weekly* (Fashion Police), *Cosmopolitan, Marie Claire, Seventeen,* and alternative mags like *Bust* and *Bitch* and on MTV. She contributed to the anthology *Body Outlaws: Rewriting the Rules of Beauty and Body Image* (Seal Press), and her essay "Big Mouth: Women & Appetite" was published in *The Modern Jewish Girl's Guide to Guilt* (Dutton). Check out her introduction in *Big Girl Knits: 25 Big, Bold Projects Shaped for Real Women with Real Curves* (Potter Craft). Go to www.wendyshanker.com for more info.

Size: XXL

Lauren R. Weinstein is a cartoonist. Her most recent book, *Girl Stories,* was published by Henry Holt and received two ALA nominations. Currently, Lauren teaches drawing and cartooning to children and adults at the 92nd Street Y, Parsons School of Design, and the School of Visual Arts. In 2003, she was the recipient of the Xeric Grant, allowing her to self-publish her first book, *Inside Vineyland.* In 2004, she received the Ignatz Award for "Promising New Talent." Her comics and illustrations have appeared in *The New York Times, Glamour, McSweeney's, LA*

Weekly, The Chicago Reader, Kramer's Ergot, and Seattle's *The Stranger.* Currently she is working on the sequel to *Girl Stories,* tentatively entitled *Calamity.* Her sci-fi fantasy comic entitled *The Goddess of War* came out in February 2008 from Picturebox.

Size: M

About the Editor

Marissa Walsh is the author of *A Field Guide to High School* and editor of the anthology *Not Like I'm Jealous or Anything: The Jealousy Book*. A former children's book editor, she lives in New York City and wears a lot of black.

Size: L

No, this book does not make you look fat.